Ella Maria Baker

Put in His Thumb and Pulled Out a Plum

Stories for a Christmas Pie

Ella Maria Baker

Put in His Thumb and Pulled Out a Plum
Stories for a Christmas Pie

ISBN/EAN: 9783743386761

Manufactured in Europe, USA, Canada, Australia, Japa

Cover: Foto ©Andreas Hilbeck / pixelio.de

Manufactured and distributed by brebook publishing software (www.brebook.com)

Ella Maria Baker

Put in His Thumb and Pulled Out a Plum

PUT IN HIS THUMB

AND

PULLED OUT A PLUM

STORIES FOR A CHRISTMAS PIE

BY

ELLA M. BAKER

Author of "SOLDIER AND SERVANT," "CLOVER LEAVES," ETC.

BOSTON

D. LOTHROP AND COMPANY

FRANKLIN STREET, CORNER OF HAWLEY

Press of Rockwell and Churchill
39 Arch St., Boston.

CONTENTS.

iii.

CONTENTS.

ILLUSTRATIONS.

v.

PUT IN HIS THUMB AND PULLED OUT A PLUM.

CHAPTER I.

ABOUT THE RICHEST GIRL IN TOWN.

"SHE is the richest girl in town!"

Rite Hollis, overhearing somebody say this, half aloud, turned and looked after the young girl who, soft with her silks and furs and feathers as a puff of thistle-down, fluttered out of Schaffer's and away to the sleigh in waiting before the door.

Well, it was a pretty sight.

Miss Maud Sylverner had the pink-and-white face and the fine soft hair that made you think of an apple blossom in a haze. Rich

7

draperies and floating plumes became her as well as its fluted velvet case becomes any jewel.

She had her arms full of bundles — such delightful, seductive-looking bundles as always come from Schaffer's. That largest one, with the square, angular outlines, was of course some picture, thought Rite, destined to make another window, as it were, let into my lady's chamber wall. But what manner of elegant trinkets might be enclosed in those smaller wrappings, with the rosy strings knotted about the firm, white paper, was left in delicious uncertainty. Delicious, because Rite enjoyed it.

Ah! a quaint little woman this was. I want to tell you about her. Just now she was out on one of her most extravagant shopping tours.

The richest girl in the town. That is what *I* call *her* — Rite Hollis.

She lived in "the old Audrey Place," but not because it was her father's property. He

was only hired to live there, and keep from
going to utter ruin, in its fallen fortunes, the
house that had been grand and gay and full
of happy people in its day. Now the hedges
were overgrown; some of the gates, never
opened, had wayward woodbine woven in many
a thickness about the rusty latch; a woful look
of decay had settled over the once handsome
buildings, and the broad lawn, with its elms
and shrubberies, was tangled and neglected.

Nor were the many apartments within, though
stately still, furnished and decorated fitly
as of old. Instead, many were unoccupied,
and there was a deprecating air about the
Hollis's simple furniture, which sparsely varie-
gated the bare house, as if to say, "I know
I am out of place in such fine company.
Pray excuse me!"

None of the rooms looked empty to Rite,
though her mother said, on wet nights, when
the wind was high, that so much unoccupied
space made her feel nervous and timid.

Rite had often wandered, since they came, two years ago, all over the house, studying the views from every window, fitting a history to every room, and imagining all about the former occupants of each. She had time for this because her life was so isolated. The Audrey Place was on an old, aristocratic street, where the neighbors were not likely to notice this humble family. The father was a reserved and quiet man; the mother never very strong. That made no difference about her being the "very best mother in all the world" to Rite. She felt so rich, so very rich, in that, to begin with.

They just grew right up together and had all things common. "The motherandI, one and indivisible, now and forever!" was one of Rite's little jokes. With innumerable mutual confidences and contrivings, they pieced each other out; managed to carry on the housework, keep big Lynde and small Dolly in jackets and petticoats, keep up father's spirits, and make a Home of it all.

The mother had so many sick days that to
do all this, rather stinted Rite on her "out-cf-
door-drinkings," as she called them, but then
she learned to make all the more of what she
could have.

After the house was put in order of a morning, and she hurried off to the Academy,
how she kept her sharp young eyes open all
the way to spy out any chance bit of fun, adventure or oddity.   These she called her
"Views A-Foot," and she saved them up to
relate at tea-time, on purpose to get father
to laugh.

Then, quite often, returning from the afternoon session, she would walk away round by
Main and State Streets, on a "Jenny Wren
tour," so as to "take pattern and cut and
try on."   Many and many a time had she
told Dolly her favorite story about poor dear
Jenny Wren, the lame girl who had a drunken
father, and who dressed dolls for a living.
How this Jenny Wren used to take " her

carriage," as she called her crutch, and go, on gala days, to watch the fine ladies in the streets, until among them all she saw a dress that particularly pleased her. How then she would hurry home to cut and baste a doll's dress like it, and then back to make the fine lady try on—"O! and take pains about it, too!"

But, though Dolly knew the story by heart, she did not realize that her own pretty dresses and aprons, and her best-beloved Sunday-school hat were all contrived by Rite in something the same way. For, when that worried middle wrinkle began to come in the tired mother's forehead, when a dress must be "made over" so frugally, or a new one developed from a scant pattern, did Rite buy the best fashion-book, as the Sylverners would have done? No; for there were Main and State Streets full of models, and admission free. She would catch sight there of a new style for trimming, or a bright idea for cutting, that would just fit in and help out, and then carry it merrily away home, to be altered or adapted with the famous, ready *motherandI* tact.

And when it came to buying cambric facings, maybe, or the nine needful buttons, with Dolly in a state of great elation holding fast by one hand, such relish had Rite, while she herself matched and selected, in quietly watching critical customers at the counter near hers turn over silks, laces and costly trimmings, that it gave her a sense of part ownership, and she would walk away with her one meek, round parcel, not a bit envious, but with a mischievous, Jenny Wren sort of feeling that the grand ladies had been shopping for her, too, and never dreamed of it!

Another way she had was to go out calling, after her own peculiar fashion.

She might be, in point of fact, on some errand about a pound of tea, or a book to be returned to the Library; but she would go round through Arlington Street, and come back by

Tilaston. That showed her the finest places in the city, and, if this russet-clad maid did not walk up the granite steps and send in her card, she perhaps gained more pleasure out of her calls than they did always receive who went through the usual ceremonies.

A fresh enthusiasm and a warm delight came to her as she caught glimpses of laces and velvets, of pictures, books and conservatories. She would dream out the characters and circumstances of the inmates, till a sense of being intimate and confidential possessed her. Who could gainsay her in this innocent liberty? This was one of her ways of being rich.

Sometimes she preferred to stay in the busier streets, among the shifting throngs, and make it a "getting acquainted" time, when she could watch and study the hurrying people, choosing and rejecting them according to her fancy.

There was one pleasure which Rite made a great deal of. Her father was sexton of

All Saints, the oldest church in the whole
city, and he liked to have Rite go with him
when there was to be a wedding that Dolly
would like to see, or when he had something
to do in the high belfry.

Rite loved dearly to climb up with him,
far, far up beside the great bell.

"This is my bird-journey, father," she said
one day, "and it lasts me a long while."

Then both were silent, gazing out on miles
of roofs, towers and spires, the river shining
near, the lake shining far, and beyond all a
glorious sunset burning out in vanishing gold
and red.

"But O, father!" said Rite at last, with a
long sigh, "what a little, *little* bit of a thing
it does make me feel!"

A white dove slowly fluttered across the
tower and walked fearlessly about its dizzy
rim, catching the last warm rays of the sinking sun upon its snowy wings. It made Rite
seem to herself still more insignificant to see

the bird so at home where her head was dizzy.

Just then a tiny mouse dodged by and dived into a hole. Somehow that brought the contented look back to Rite's awed face, and, while she stood waiting for her father below, she thought, looking up at the stained window where the Christ held out his hand to the sinking Peter, "After all, I'm not afraid to be such a small thing in such a big world. There's a Hand over me, too, mouse as I am."

There was something beautiful in those quiet, waiting moments there by the stained window — she often went into the church just for that. "To listen," she said to herself, "and hush."

You remember that a holy man says, "Ah, how few souls there are still enough to hear God speak."

That same night poor Dolly waked her sister up, crying.

"O Rite!" she moaned, "I've got a crazy tooth! a crazy tooth!"

Mother must not be disturbed if Rite could help it, so she doctored the naughty tooth with all her skill, and then, cuddling Dolly close, hurried to soothe her with a story.

"There, dear, now hark!" she began; "I'll tell you how a mouse got a Christmas dinner.

"She was a mother mouse, and she lived quite close to a big Bell. It was in the family to be very saving, and they managed somehow into the winter till it grew late and bitter and cold, and the mother mouse fell sick. Alas! now came sad, starving times for the baby mice. What could the mother mouse do?

"One day she ran feebly up to the great Bell and said, 'O, Bell, we're starving to death!'

"Not a word answered the Bell.

"'O, surely, Bell,' begged she, quite bold

with hunger, 'you with your great, strong voice can call somebody to help us!'

"Still the grand Bell was silent.

"Perhaps the mouse thought the Bell was too proud and fine to care, but you and I know that he couldn't move his own tongue by himself.

"At anyrate the mouse crawled away and lay down again."

"Like little Samuel," put in Dolly, in a voice that was forgetting to be plaintive.

"Well; when the sexton came next to ring the Bell something was wrong.

"'Why, what has the old Bell done to itself?' asked he; 'and almost time to ring for Christmas! This will never do!'

"So he went clambering up with workmen to see what was the matter. O, they didn't know there was a mouse's Christmas dinner in the business.

"But the starving thing was so bold with want that she crept out to them. One man put forth his foot to kick her away. But the other had a little girl at home, and he thought, 'Now this will make a Christmas story for her.' So he said, 'No, let it be; it's starving; and it can't be the Lord's choice that any sort of creature should starve to death at Christmas-time.'

"Then he pulled out what was left of his own lunch from his pocket, and the next time the old Bell rang the mother mouse and the baby mousies were nibbling away at their Christmas dinner.

"I don't know how many Christmas dinners were eaten that day in the city; but just to think, that, amongst all of them, God hadn't forgotten to give the mice theirs!"

"Do you think He really cared?" asked Dolly, in a sleepy voice.

"Of course I do!" Rite answered, boldly; "and here's a verse that I'll teach you to-morrow.

"'He prayeth best who loveth best
　All things both great and small;
For the dear God who loveth us —'"

I doubt if Dolly heard the rest of the verses, but Rite could not get to sleep again so easily. She lay thinking and thinking. At last she crept noiselessly out of bed, and turned over once more the contents of a certain mysterious drawer which she kept locked. In it, carefully folded, lay a new shirt which she had made for her father, a comforter of her knitting for Lynde, a made-over doll for the small sister, and some afternoon aprons for mother. Rite smoothed these things down lovingly, but she sighed a little, and made up her mind to go shopping to-morrow.

So here she was, this day before Christmas Eve, when our story begins. She had roamed all down Asterisk Street, and chosen the prettiest carpet in Bee & Bonnet's window, just the thing for mother's room. She had stood delighted before the florist's window, and made up vivid word-pictures of it to take home to her mother, for her mother used to live in the country.

She had decided on the very shawl, soft and warm, which she would best like to give the mother for a Christmas present, the very set of furs which would have been ecstasy to Dolly. As to Lynde, she knew what he wanted most; already he made a Genii of his jack-knife, and she had noticed a set of tools that would just suit him.

And now she had paused with the throng in front of Schaffer's, where there was so much to attract in statuary, or pictures, or Sorrento carvings, that it always sent her home with heart full if not hands; and I should just like to know which is better! Some of the pictures would suggest bits of stories to tell to Dolly; some of them would help her out for composition days; and only to hear about them was change and rest and pleasure to the invalid mother, half for her own sake and half for Rite's.

I don't pretend that Rite was at all extraordinary; but she had the real wealth of a contented spirit, and that faculty for making the most of things which can redeem any life from poverty.

It had seemed pretty hard last night that she could not see the heart's desires of those dearest to her satisfied at this Christmas season; but now her shopping excursion was making her blithe again. Surely the evergreens that Lynde had been away out on the Lower Road to get were finer than those for sale on the street. She had seen a rustic frame at Greenough's that she was sure she could copy. And how the sleigh-bells rang out! How merry everybody looked, and what odd packages they carried!

There was a picture of the Christmas Bell which had just caught Rite's eye, and she was saying to herself, "How father would like this for a Christmas present! I'll choose that for him!" when those words reached her, "She is the richest girl in town," and then she watched Miss Sylverner away.

The Sylverners went to All Saints, and their grounds joined the old Audrey Place. Rite liked the Sylverner house better than any she knew. It had a happy, hospitable look, and a large, old-fashioned garden, with odd-shaped, box-bordered beds, full not only of fashionable beauties, but real old countrified flowers, 'that pressed out through the fence to beckon at passers-by. The people had a habit of leaving shutters unbarred and curtains rolled up, and almost always, at twilight, music came floating out thence. To Rite, walking slowly past at such times, and listening, this was better than the opera. She never had been to a real, grand concert in her life, nor played on anything better than their ancient melodeon, with its perpetual cold in the head. But not stacks of new music

could have given more real enjoyment than
did the snatches and strains which Rite's
quick ear thus caught and carried, to repro-
duce again as she went singing about the
great empty house.

When, of an evening, she put all her innocent heart into the air of some new song, till
father looked up and beat time, with a smile,
till Lynde came and stood beside her, proud
of the ready knack which could so easily
learn, and mother dropped her work, with
the rested look in her soft eyes which Rite
knew so well, and watched for so constantly,
—this was one of the times when the child
best realized her riches, and found the giving
of them more blessed than even the receiving.

It was fast getting dusk, and Lynde came
springing down the long street to meet Rite,
as she reached the Sylverner's corner.

"Merry Christmas, ma'am!" he cried, coming up full of sly mischief, and pinching her
arm. "See the wreaths in all the windows,

Rite! Isn't it gay? The Sylverner's house is lit all over!"

"O, but the blinds are shut where the picture is!" suddenly exclaimed Rite, in a disappointed tone.

"The picture?" queried Lynde, "what picture do you mean?"

"Haven't you ever noticed it? It shows quite plainly by lamp-light. A portrait of a beautiful woman. Why, I dream about her at night sometimes, she fascinates me so! Lynde, I wish you could see her. How very bright the light is behind those shut blinds!"

"There must be a side window to that room," said Lynde, his curiosity being roused by Rite's enthusiasm for the picture; "let us walk up our drive-way, Rite. It curves so that I shouldn't wonder if it would come quite near that window, and maybe the blinds have been left open on that side."

He pushed open a rusty gate laboriously, and Rite ran merrily up the overgrown drive-way, with its artful curves and windings.

"What a hurry you are in!" Lynde called after her; "I do believe you'll have to come and help me push this gate back, after all."

Suddenly Rite's voice came back to him.

Was it her voice? It was not so much that it was raised loud, but there was such a thrill of alarm and excitement in it that Lynde said afterwards, "It burned like cold iron."

"Ring the door-bell, Lynde — quick! quick! That room is all on fire!"

CHAPTER II.

"I NEVER shall forget it as long as I live!" declared Maud Sylverner, in a shaking voice, "the way that girl looked, Cousin Red! I've seen tragedy for once and for all. There we sat at the long table — dinner was very late — all of us younger folks so full of fun, between the people that had come and the people that were coming, and yet rather held in, you know, by great-uncle Brederode, because he is so much of a stranger, and a writer and traveller, too. And

27

he was just saying, 'As I heard the bell toll there at Lima, because the church rocked so with the earthquake'—when a door burst open, and there stood this strange girl, with, of all things in the world, the great picture of Agatha Sylverner in her arms, and a face like death!

"I couldn't have told, myself, whether it was Peru or the Judgment Day. We all sprang and rushed, and I had a confused idea that the picture of the Christmas Bell, I had just bought, must be saved at all risks. But I don't pretend to be certain of anything till you came hurrying in at the hall-door, with your grandmotherly shawl on, and somebody said, 'Why, Maud! how long are you going to hug that picture?'

"Then I realized that Rite Hollis was lying on my bed, with some burns and bruises, that we were all together, guests and all, that nothing was saved unhurt from the drawing-room but the ·portrait, and that it wasn't worth while for me to clutch my poor, smoked 'Christmas Bell' any longer.

"But O, Cousin Red! a houseful of company, and no Christmas tree!"

"All the presents weren't on, though?" questioned one of the eager girls.

"No, we waited for cousin Red to finish, and the rest, too, who are coming to-morrow."

"But how could it have —"

"Girls," said Mrs. Sylverner, coming in hastily, "does anybody know where Ronald is?"

Nobody noticed the long slit in her hastily-pinned-up silk, nor the comical sooty spot which tipped her dignified nose.

For, surely, where *was* Ronald?

There was a sudden dispersion; Mrs. Sylverner called Maud, suggested how late it had grown, to the others, and turned to look for the latest arrival, cousin Red, whom she had scarcely greeted. But cousin Red had vanished in her own noiseless, quick way.

Ronald was a pet of hers. She had swiftly gone down-stairs, and opened the first door. All was still in the dark library, as she flashed her little bed-room candle about. Book-cases up and down, portraits, portfolios, bronzes; nobody under the sofas, nobody under the heavy easy-chairs, nobody in the little closet.

"Ronald! Ronald!"

At her voice he would surely answer.

No answer. She went out and closed the door, carefully shielding her candle.

Across to the sitting-room. The lifted light, flickering full on the broad mirrors, and bringing out clearly her own image, gave her a second's sensation of awe. What if there were a mirror of the spirit to reflect thoughts? What if, sometimes, we were forced to hold the 'torch and come face to face with ourselves in that?

Here all was in order, all undisturbed.

"Ronald! Ronald, dear!"

No reply.

She looked in at the music-room, but it was plainly untenanted. She opened the drawing-room door. The long room showed blackened and desolate, with all its recesses laid open, quite empty but for broken furniture, splintered glass, crumbling shapes of holly, and such remnants of the feast of Fire. No one here.

The dining-room was littered with napkins dropped anywhere. A chair had fallen over, which cousin Red mechanically set up again with precision. There a fallen spoon, here a splintered goblet. Flowers glowed on the table. Fruit was arrayed on the side-board, its elaborate piles quite unbroken among the silver. Only the cook haunted this room. She was sure that she had not seen Ronald " this hull 'orrid night."

The other children are at last soothed to sleep in the nursery. Cousin Red kisses a face or two softly, and, though she is anxious as she flits on, cannot help thinking how picturesque the succession of contrasting rooms is.

For more doors open as her light foot passes, and anxious, pretty faces, above bright flannel dressing-gowns, or white, ruffled sacques, challenge her. "Nobody in our rooms. We've looked everywhere, closets and all."

"Try the attic," suggests one, as Maud and her mother appear, having searched in all out-of-the-way corners. The three tapers go flickering and fluttering through the clutter of huddling furniture, boxes, chests, frames with faces to the wall, piles of newspapers, festoons wrought by persevering, irrepressible spiders.

"I'm afraid he must have strayed off with some of the people who gathered," said Mrs. Sylverner, thoroughly distressed.

But cousin Red remembered one place more.

"Don't disturb grandma," Mrs. Sylverner had said; nevertheless cousin Red ventured softly to steal in where grandma, worn out, had at last fallen asleep. Shading her glimmering candle with her hand, she peered sharply into every tuck-away place there. Now grandma's old-fashioned bed, whose four posts uplifted four dark carved acorns, had a white valance falling to the floor. When, with a careful hand, cousin Red lifted this, she was sure that something darker than the darkness lay in a forlorn heap at that farthest, coldest corner. Yes, something stirred as she let the light shine in; Ronald's face, red with sleep, muddy with smeary tears, and startling with round, black, frightened eyes, certainly looked up to her one second, then was quickly turned to the wall again, like any tiny, huddling wild thing, surprised in the woods.

Not a word was said. Cousin Red gathered the shivering bundle up into her arms somehow, and swiftly carried it away into her own room. But before she could hurry to tell that the missing boy was found, he burst into such great, breathless, convulsive sobs, that it seemed as though he would lose his breath.

"I thought — I'd just — light a few," he gasped, "for fun, — and it all — burst up! Don't — don't tell! Don't bring me! They'll put me in prison. They do, for burning up houses! O, please don't!"

It is pitiful to see a child in pain and terror, and Ronald was in a wild agony of dread that cousin Red really couldn't stand.

"My darling," said she, very tenderly, yet firmly, "cousin Red won't let anybody hurt you. I won't tell anybody till you say I may, Ronald, nor let anybody see you till you say so. Don't cry any more. You shall sleep with me right here to-night — hush dear! — and I'll make it all right. Now wait for me one minute."

She carried the news to the disturbed household, obtained Mrs. Sylverner's leave to manage Ronald, and sent her to take needed rest, then went back.

Ronald had crept away into the darkest

Little Ronald is miserable.

corner, and crouched there, still trembling with cold and fear, his face to the wall again. He moaned something about how "It all burst right up!" and "The Christmas tree gone!" and "Jumped out of the window and ran away!"

"Come right out of that corner, little Jack Horner!" cried cousin Red, in a hearty, merry tone, that did much to persuade the child that the world would really go round just the same as ever after all this dreadful loss and naughtiness. Though he still begged to stay in the corner, how comforting and restful it was, after all, to be brought out of it by a strong hand, undressed and laid in a soft, clean bed, and to be getting warm between the blankets.

Wrapped in "the grandmotherly shawl," cousin Red sat down on the bed, and took hold of his hand, and Ronald owned all up to her.

How for fun and curiosity he had climbed

in at the side window, which somebody had left unfastened, knowing that the drawing-room door was locked. How he had matches in his pocket, and wanted to see how one or two of the tapers would look lit up. But how he was frightened almost to death when it blazed up, and so he jumped out of the open window, and ran away for fear of prison, and then couldn't think where to go, and came back and hid under grandma's bed.

O, dear! wouldn't there be any Christmas now? *Would* they put him in prison? What would papa and mamma say?

"Dear! dear! what shall I do?" sobbed the little rogue, whose mischief had found him out, and was more than his childish heart could bear.

But cousin Red spoke up briskly. It was her crisp, quick, unsentimental way.

"Well, Ronald, you're in a fix. You're in a corner sure enough, my little Jack Horner. But you've been punished. You're sorry.

Then it's no use to *stay* in the corner. Particularly, with your face to the wall. Remember that! It's no use, *ever*, to stay of your own accord in a corner, with your face to the wall. There's a way out of your corner, and there isn't but one. Just be a man, and go right away as soon as you wake up in the morning, to papa and mamma, and own right up, honest and sorry, every single thing. Then it will all come right."

O dear, dear, dear! Ronald couldn't. He couldn't bear to see anybody, or have anybody see him. Everybody would hate him! He'd burned up the beautiful Christmas tree, full of presents. Oh! let him have any little bit of a corner to stay in that was out of sight, and he'd do anything else.

That Corner of his was just the one thing, though, that cousin Red couldn't think of letting him have. But he'd feel better about it if he waited till to-morrow. So now he must go to sleep, and cousin Red would not let anything hurt him.

"Only remember, dear," she said, "just this time of year, long ago, the Friend we had been naughtiest to, came to forgive us and make a way for us out of all our troubles. Now, because it is that time, your father and mother will be glad to let you out of your troubles, I am sure. Try and see."

Then she soothed Ronald till he fell asleep, exhausted, but rid of that dreadful feeling about there being no way out.

No one slept very soundly in the house that night.

Rite Hollis caught only snatches of disturbed repose, between some pain and discomfort, her fears that mother would be worried, and the strange sensation it was to be lying in Maud Sylverner's dainty bed, among so many strange, pretty things, the gas burning low, and Maud stealing in at intervals from the dressing-room. She had insisted on having a couch there, and taking care of Rite herself. For Maud had a generous, big heart, and out of it quite won Rite's ready love by bewitching, little matronly attentions, and all the serious, steady airs of a responsible nurse.

But if you suppose that the catastrophe was going to be allowed to spoil all the Christmas fun, you are much mistaken.

O dear, no! So many delightful people, so many happy, ingenious young folks, were not met together for that. Never mind about the Christmas tree, but as to the Christmas Night party, who'd complain of bare floors in the drawing-room? They would bring in the woods, so that it might seem like a dancing-hall laid in a pine forest. There was nothing left now to be spoiled by nails or litter.

Luckily "the lion," uncle Brederode, had been invited to drive with the Mayor. The New York cousins were wild to go with the party which rallied promptly for gathering evergreens in the woods, and to undertake the decoration of the drawing-room. There were country cousins who wanted to do a little Christmas shopping, and set forth gaily, led by Mrs. Sylverner. Some begged for the fun of helping in the kitchen about the plum-pudding and Christmas-pie work. The Bride was coming by the afternoon train — she was sure to be charming. And then, there was cousin Red.

In different tones of self-gratulation, everybody was saying, "There is cousin Red!"

She was one of those people rare to meet, and difficult to describe, about whom we fall back on the indefinite word "fascinating." She could hold people spellbound by her music; she could read and mimic exquisitely; she could talk so that no other entertainment seemed as charming. And she seemed always to know just what to do for herself and other people. So that all her friends and relatives were apt to rely upon her, declaring that she was a "host in herself."

The Host it was, then, that scapegrace Ronald had on his side, that bright, frosty morning, when he awoke to face his predicament. The Host it was who reasoned and persuaded till he made up his mind bravely, and, with small, brown hands clenched tight together, from the effort he was making, went straight to mamma's room, before the house was awake, with his penitent confession.

The consciousness of the Host it was which nerved him to take his shame-faced place beside her at the breakfast-table, and have the meeting with all the company over at once.

Ah! it was so much better than it would have been to stay in the Corner. There isn't any other way than to step right out of it, is there? Not any other good, brave, manly way.

And let us all lay to heart one thing. Let us never remember against anybody who has got out of a Corner that he has been in it. Let us not lay it up against him; but forget it and help him to forget it.

Now Ronald, handling his fork rather

uncertainly, and afraid his eyes were red still, felt in his shivering soul that the disgrace of the Corner was on him yet, in — well, uncle Brederode's eyes, for instance, when he looked at him so severely from his tall man's height. And it hurt.

But then almost everybody took pains *not* to look any more awful than usual, or else forgot, in the most encouraging way, even to take pains. And cousin Red treated him just like a man. So Ronald took heart not to look back at the dark Corner.

Now the good times began. It was in the air of the house, rightly named *Bien-venu*. It was open all over, and everybody was to do just what he or she liked best.

On the Sylverner side and on the Rodney side there were hosts of relatives, who, for grandma's sake, and the glad, open-handed hospitality of the family custom, were always mustered, so far as possible, to this yearly assembling.

Some of the girls were making a ring-cake, with delicious nibblings, weighings and measurings. Rustling and laughing went on over mysterious packages, for, since there was no Christmas tree, each was to bestow the intended gifts as best suited his taste. The door-bell rang in an erratic manner. Somebody was dashing off Christmas Carols at the piano.

Maud feared that Rite would get lonesome, or be neglected. But she need not have feared. After it was all understood and explained, after Mrs. Sylverner had thanked her, with genuine heartiness and dignified simplicity, for the warning which had saved the house, after Rite's word had gone home and her mother's had come back, they all put Rite quite at ease. She was like the mouse she had called herself, looking on at the banquet from her nest in the wall. Only all the banqueters were so delicately mindful of her. Besides the bruise, and the burn, and the slight sprain she had received in their service, it was remembered, after the excitement was over, how heroically she had worked, scarcely noticed while the fire lasted. Only her daring, at the early moment when she saw the flames through the window Ronald had left open, indeed, could have saved the portrait they were all so proud of; and grandma herself came in on Maud's arm, to insist on thanking Rite in person.

Altogether, the girls quite gloried in Rite, made a great heroine of her, and were delighted with her timid, bright ways. So the ring-cake party would have her taste the batter when it had been stirred stiff with fruit, and nibble bits of the citron. The party from the woods brought her a bunch of wintergreen and princess pine.

Maud administered the salves and such alleviations as had been prescribed, repeating meanwhile all that was nicest or funniest in the goings-on, and Mrs. Sylverner saw that she lacked nothing which kindly tact could suggest. They could not let her go home, Mrs. Sylverner said, till after Christmas. That burn must heal before she exposed herself at all to the air. But Rite's brother must come in often, and they would contrive that she should see her father and mother, too, before the day was out.

Rite, knowing her mother's invalid ways, and her father's reserved habits, had some private doubts of this, but such considerate kindness was very soothing. So, in her own contented way, she dwelt but little, after that, on whatever pain or weariness last night's mishaps had caused her, but lay with smiles on her pale face, making the most of all this wealth of pleasant things around her, and thinking how wonderful it all was to be sure — a real story happened to her at last, and no making up, nor imagining about it!

CHAPTER III.

THE Host was assembled by herself in Maud's dressing-room, biting her lips, and tapping her foot in its trim French slipper. She had forgotten all about Rite, who could not help seeing her through the open door, but lay quite still.

However, cousin Red never stayed in a perplexity long, and presently the foot stopped tapping. She spied Rite, and, approaching her, said cheerily:

"Aha! I forgot there was somebody in

48

Maud's room when I popped into it so. You are Rite Hollis, I'm sure. Well, I'm — suppose we say The Man in the Moon; and I wonder now, if I inquire the way to Norwich, couldn't you be so obliging as to direct me, Miss Rite?"

Of course Rite hadn't the least idea to whom she was talking; but she answered archly, for the lady's manner was so piquant and gracious that it was infectious:

"I'd be very glad to play guide-post if I could, only you must put me where the roads fork, first."

Then cousin Red proceeded to explain:

It appeared that there was sore affliction in the nursery. The Sylverners, minor, could not at first realize the magnitude of last night's calamity.

But when at last they did realize that the long-anticipated Christmas tree was finally and fatally lost to them, that there was no chance for the sublime sight they had looked forward

to, this year, it was too much for their bereaved souls.

O! to think that so many pretty things
had been burned up with the tree! To think
that Walter's coveted silver watch might have
been there! That Nina's splendid promised
doll probably was! And Ronald was somehow
to blame. Nina and Walter would not speak
to Ronald; the sound of weeping and wail-
ing made the air dismal. There they were,
and so damp that cousin Red declared she
dared not stay in their neighborhood, for
fear she'd catch cold.

But that soft-hearted woman, after all, felt
a sympathetic tear in one eye at sight of the
children's woes and disappointment, and after
she had slightly assuaged the flood with sugar-
plums, had gone off by herself to think of
some way in which to make it up to the
sufferers.

"I won't have anybody feeling bad around
me at Christmas time!" said she, "and there's

poor little Jack Horner snubbed and low-spirited enough again, too, and his presents gone by the fire just as much as any-body's."

"Jack Horner?" queried Rite, beginning to look knowing. Then, as cousin Red went on to explain why Jack Horner, Rite cried out:

"If Jack Horner, why not Jack Horner

"'Eating a Christmas pie?'"

and they both clapped their hands together, as the idea glanced into cousin Red's quick brain in a flash, almost before it left Rite's.

"Well, you are a guide-post worth hav-ing!" exclaimed cousin Red, lightly pinching Rite's index finger. "Of course! A glorious Christmas Pie, in the biggest of all chopping-bowls, everything to delight the little people under the cover, and then the surprise and the glory of putting in a thumb! It must be served up this very evening, and I must go straight to the cooking, now."

"What plotting is this!" demanded Maud, coming in upon them with the semi-sobbing Nina dragging after her.

Cousin Red, with a radiant face, waltzed her off to explain, while Rite coaxed Nina to her, and beguiled away the tears with stories about Dolly. In fact, the weather changed about this time among the nursery folks. It became known that there *was* going to be something for them that evening.

Cousin Red said so, and Miss Maudie said so, too!

They called their elder sister Miss Maudie, in a funny little fashion which they had probably caught from nurse and the servants.

Well, it came evening ever so fast, and at early lamp-lighting the household were all gathered together. It seemed as though a prettier sight never showed under Christmas holly. For there was grandma in her black silk, snowy cap, and the soft lace under-hand-kerchief, which she always wore folded at the neck.

There was the bride, very winning and shy, and certainly very lovely. There was the Sylverner college boy, now one of the dignitaries of the family, with his grand airs —but the boy would show through! There was the maiden aunt, apt to be wanted by everybody at once, the one who knew all about the new books, the new stitches in fancy-work, the new games, and the cutting and making of any known garment this side of Paris, or, for aught I know, of Paradise.

The dear maiden aunt! All the love-stories in the family were told to her first, and she always laughed and cried over them as if the story were her own. If anybody was sick she was the one who always hurried to help. If the great grief of a last good-by came into the family, nobody knew so well how to speak or to be silent, to comfort and to quiet, and to take fast hold of the mourner, as aunt Moneywort did.

Uncle Brederode was the traveller. Of course he was something to be proud of. You remember his books, of course. Besides having been all over the world, he was a student and a thinker. Only, he had been abroad so long that he seemed like a stranger this first Christmas after his return. Then the New York cousins were looking their prettiest, and, really, the country cousins were not very much outshone; and there was one who sketched beautifully, and another one who wrote for the *Exeter*.

Rite was present, having been brought down, with Maud's best pink wrapper, with its swan's-down trimmings, on, and ensconced in the easiest chair. Her father and mother, Lynde, and even Dolly, were all around her, Mrs. Sylverner and cousin Red having managed to overrule all their shy and delicate scruples, in some manner incomprehensible to Rite.

The hospitality of the house was simply unlimited, and Rite had never seen its like. The name of English hospitality is well known, and so, in our country, is Western hospitality. Here the two were put together; the Rodneys were Western people, while the Sylverners came of English stock.

Rite's loving eyes followed "Miss Maudie," and to her, nobody in the room could surpass her new friend. She was shaped in the tiniest mould that you might see in a life-time, perhaps, for a woman full-grown, yet exquisitely perfect, and in every appointment as fastidiously exact as such a fairy could afford to be. Her graceful, accented manners, the picturesque fitness and harmony of her person, from the tip of her wavy, gold-brown hair to the rosette of her Cinderella slippers, made her charming to everybody who saw her. Maud's "particular friend," who would be present at the party, said that there never could have been a fairy queen half so lovely as mortal Maud.

And the baby! Bless me! the idea of my forgetting to say that the last new baby was there, kept up beyond her usual bed-time in honor of the Christmas season, and grandma's seventy-eighth birth-day. Yes, that dear old lady had actually added to the obligations of her descendants by appropriating Christmas Eve for her birthday! Her little grandchildren had been heard to say grandma had the best birthday of anybody — but of course grandma ought to have. Only they did wish they could have had a chance to pick it out first!

Mrs. Sylverner was the perfection of hostesses, shining upon everybody, and directing without dictating. Her husband had words in season for all, and cousin Red just scintillated.

She had uncle Brederode talking his very best right away; bestowed queer, significant

nods and smiles upon Rite; had a pat or a
pinch ready for anybody who would feel better
for it; and, above all, she made fun for the
children, and somehow turned it into *their*
merrymaking, with riddles, and the maiden
aunt games, and bits of songs, and some short
Christmas stories, "told small," as the children
begged, and told as only cousin Red could
do it.

She had the children all about her, and some
of them had their dolls, too. Ronald sat beside her, in a high chair, that had been dex-
terously pushed into a corner.

Just when the frolic and the fun were at
their very tip-top feather, and Mr. Sylverner
had let off his contribution to their entertainment, a very gay, ingenious toy-balloon, which
first soared up into the high room, over the
children's heads, then, floating down, collapsed
in their midst with a flash and a bang, while
down tumbled, not the balloon only, but
showers of French *bon-bons* and Christmas

mottoes, — just then, before they had time to scramble, clang, clang, clang went the great front door-bell. Upon that, every bell in the house began to ring, too, the loud dinner-bell, the little silver bell, the servant's bell, and then the tinkling of sleigh-bells came bounding, bouncing in, and (who don't know Santa Claus by sight? You children have all seen him nowadays) the great, fur-clad, puffing, wheezing figure rushed up to that corner chair, and, with a loud, jubilant stamp and flourish, dumped down, if you'll believe me, an enormous snow-white pie before Ronald's chair !

"Christmas Pie for Jack Horner!" he roared, in such a voice as you'd suppose Santa Claus to have. "Best compliments of Santa Claus' cook!" By this time he had jingled back to the door. "Merry Christmas to all, and to all a good-night!" sounded back, fainter and further along the hall, and with a frantic clatter of bells he was gone.

"Jack Horner." puts in his thumb.

But it was not a dream, for he had left the Christmas Pie.

Ronald was like to tumble out of his chair with amazement. Somebody laughed. Somebody cried. Uncle Brederode shouted,

"Hurrah! hurrah! hurrah!"

Yes, he actually did. Three times. He was as much surprised as anybody.

There was a great clapping of hands, and everybody pressed round the Pie. Even Rite, forgetting herself, tried to start up from her chair.

O! it was a magnificent Pie! Such round, white sides, such deep bowels, such ornaments of holly, such lettering, fat and jolly, that said,

> " Put in your thumb
> Pull out a plum !"

Well, somehow, they stopped laughing, stopped crying, stopped cheering; cousin Red managed. Like the five and twenty blackbirds, all the

children huddled chattering round. Somehow
the cover was taken off, and little Jack
Horner bidden to put in his thumb.

What layers of little parcels were carefully
crammed into that tight-packed middle!

Ah! what might, and what might not be
hidden under the tissue papers, all scattered
over with raisins and candies! In fear and
awe the trembling Jack put in his thumb
and pulled out — a tiny box marked "*Nina.*"
In it lay a turquoise-blue locket which brought
Nina's heart up to her throat with ecstasy.

The next pulling brought a marvelous pearl-
handled knife for Walter, and lo! next came
something for Jack Horner, himself, and then
the most captivating little ring for Amy
Rodney.

Thumb after thumb began to steal into the
Pie. Plum after plum emerged. Was ever
such rapture? Dolly, at Rite's elbow, could
say nothing but "O! O! O!" for her mouth
was full of sugar-plums, and her hands were

full of presents. Emmie was making noise
enough for two — because the doll could not
speak — over the doll's travelling-bag, her fan,
parasol, eye-glasses and seal-skin cloak. Jamie
was wild over his queer foreign toys.

O! when that Pie was opened, how they all
did begin to sing!

But it's no use for me to try to tell half
the gifts that were in it, for Jack Horner and
all the rest. People must guess.

For bed-time had to come, even on Christmas Night, even when papas and mammas
were almost as carried away with glee as
their little boys and girls. So, to quiet the
excited children, Miss Maudie led all the
small, shrill voices in some Christmas hymns,
and the room grew hushed, as thus the
listeners were reminded who was a Child
among the elders near two thousand years
ago.

Ronald really forgot all about the Corner
— what little boy wouldn't, after this? — and

cried, when they were giving and taking good-night kisses, "O, it's the best Christmas, the *best* Christmas, I ever had in my life! Ain't it, grandma? Ain't it the best Christmas *you* ever had?"

How could little Jack Horner know why grandma wiped her glasses and said, "Almost, dear, almost," instead of "Yes, yes, Ronald."

By that time he had caught the bride's eye, and was asking her:

"What was the best Christmas *you* ever had?"

Nobody could help noticing how confused and blushing the bride grew at this simple question, and kindly aunt Moneywort beckoned Ronald away.

But some whim possessed Ronald to persist with his first question, "Ain't it the best Christmas *you* ever had, aunt Moneywort?"

Aunt Moneywort did not shake her head like that and look so mysterious for nothing. Ronald, however, not satisfied with such an

answer, was in such a merry, daring mood
that he put the same question to uncle
Brederode, sitting near. Ordinarily Ronald
stood in awe of uncle Brederode, because, having overheard him called "the lion," he naturally expected him to roar, or grab up small
boys, or do something to support his character.

Now, however, uncle Brederode only smiled
and said, "I should like to tell you, sometime, my boy."

One or two other people, overhearing
Ronald's question, looked across at each other,
and smiled, in a significant manner, suggestive
of mutual understanding.

Certainly there was something tantalizing in
all this, and cousin Red did not lose a word
nor a sign of it.

"What is all this hiding of plums?" she
cried, as the children trooped away; "aunt
Moneywort, grandmother, uncle Brederode,
what nice Christmas stories are you selfishly

hiding away, to have all by yourselves, instead of sharing them with the rest of us?

"Now that you're found out, come, bring out your plums! Tell us, grandma, all about the Christmas nicer than Ronald's that you've had; and aunt Moneywort and the rest shall follow, in their turn."

"O! it's too long a story," said grandma, laughing indulgently.

"And so is mine," said aunt Moneywort.

"And I've promised Ronald that he shall hear mine," said uncle Bredcrode.

The bride only blushed deeper than ever, and said nothing, as cousin Red's eye fell on her.

Cousin Red clapped her hands softly.

"Very well, then," said she, "we'll wait for the Christmas Pie to cook. Listen: all these stories that have been hinted at shall be written out by another Christmas Eve, and then I do contract to set before the king, when we meet here again, such a dainty dish as shall surpass the Christmas Pie we've had already."

"What does the child mean?" queried grandma, placidly amused.

"A plan for next Christmas Eve, grandma. All of us good folk here, who have hinted at having had a specially good Christmas plum, shall agree to contribute the same, and we will put them all together in one generous, general Christmas Pie, for the delectation of us all! Why, I've one that I'll put in myself!"

Cousin Red always bewitched people into letting her have her own way. She infected them, too, with her own enthusiasm about it, which was better yet. Besides, people were ready for any mischief to-night. She coaxed grandma, and wheedled aunt Moneywort, and at Rite's involuntary, "O, mother — that Christmas of yours!"— set herself to win Mrs. Hollis over to her sudden scheme.

Maud agreed to write down grandma's story

for her. The guest with the skilful pencil offered to help anybody out, if desired, with her ready sketching. She was one of the Ready-to-Help family, who, thank God! are getting to keep up with the Ready-to-Halts, in point of numbers.

Long after Rite had been carried up-stairs, quite tired out, and her gentle mother had gone home, looking bright and youthful, the sounds of music and mirth went on down-stairs.

In the midst of it there was a pause; the lights were turned low. Before they had time to wonder, Mr. Sylverner came in from an adjoining room, and pushed the folding doors open as he came.

They looked through into the old dining-hall, dark now save for the moonlight, which streamed in full, as by day the sunlight could, to warm and brighten the heavy oak furniture and buff hangings, till cousin Red said "The room looked like a sleepy Maltese cat, basking in the sun."

There, in its place of honor and dignity, stood the long, old-fashioned clock that carried the moon, and had inscribed upon it the grave, resounding words composed for it by a famous Sylverner:

"I am old and gray as my face appears,
For I've walked on time for a hundred years;
Thousands have died since I begun,
Thousands will die ere my race be run.
I have buried the world, with its hopes and fears,
In my long, lone march of a hundred years."

Carefully, slowly, like a miser counting his gold pieces to make sure that the tale is full, the old clock measured out twelve strokes.

Right; none missing.

"A Merry Christmas! And God Bless Us Every One!" cried Mr. Sylverner, in a hearty voice.

Then the interchange of greetings passed around the circle, drawing them, whether they were nearly or remotely related in blood, all close together within the circle of Christmas Morning's benediction, "Peace, good will!"

The lights were out in the house, when, later, Rite started up from a doze:

" O, Miss Sylverner! listen! "

Four rich, perfectly-accorded male voices were singing the glad news without —" that once the angels sang," and the clear-sounding words seemed to fill the silent air:

> "Christians, awake! salute the happy morn,
> Whereon the Saviour of mankind was born.
> Rise to adore the mystery of love
> Which hosts of angels chanted from above;
> With them the joyful tidings first begun
> Of God incarnate and the Virgin's Son! "

CHAPTER IV.

RITE'S DIVIDENDS.

HIGH carnival held the house all Christmas day. All manner of queer presents, and all manner of dear presents, in all sorts of odd devices and comical disguises kept revealing themselves the whole day through.

The grand Christmas dinner was enjoyed with hearty zest. Uncle Brederode proved that he was not above charming his young relatives with his traveller's tales. The funny uncle told his wittiest stories. He was the man who never had escaped the nickname of

Mr. Buttonover, which one of his small nieces had given him by innocently saying, on an occasion when he told his funny stories and tried to keep his mouth straight together, that it made her think of the way a roll buttoned over at the sides.

And nobody knows how long they might have lingered at that enchanted table, had not Walter been asked by indulgent uncle Buttonover, "Won't you have more nuts?"

"No, thank you," replied that young gentleman, with an evident unwillingness that gave a pathos to the sober deliberation of his *naïve* response, "I can't. My mouth is hungry, but my stomach isn't!"

This convulsed the dinner-table; but, being voted a pretty accurate statement of the general condition, it suggested a change of occupations, and the chairs were pushed back, in the midst of jests and laughter.

It was high time, for they had the finishing touches to put to the drawing-room, and be-

sides, the girls wanted plenty of time to dress
for the party.

Rite's ankle was more painful to-day. She
could not go down, by any means; but all the
girls condoled and came to show their toilets,
Matie and Connie and Hattie and Carrie, as
well as Maud, glad to count her in. Aunt
Moneywort presided, and was looping here
and fastening there, with her mouth full of
pins, up to the last minute.

The ring-cake was cut before they went
down, too, and among the dozen girls, lo!
the ring fell to Rite. There was no cheating
about it, either. Rite felt overwhelmed, and
demurred very much; but cousin Red, queenly
in her rustling dark silk, and the coral ornaments which were her father's gift of to-day,
hushed up the protests by some of her irre-
sistible arts, and while the rest laughed and
congratulated in a merry hubbub, fitted the
ring herself on Rite's index finger, saying
"Due honors to you, trusty guide-post!"

Rite felt very happy as she lay by herself, while the sounds of mirth and music floated up from the bowery drawing-room, whose transformation had been described to her.

Among all the givings of the day she had not been forgotten by her new friends. Maud left a delicate bit of parian in her hands. Mr. Sylverner sent her a richly-bound book of poems, "with his acknowledgements." Grandma, with her own hands, brought in a work-case of Russia leather.

"O, you are all too kind!" remonstrated Rite, growing quite pink with excitement.

"Ah, dear," said grandma, "you don't know how much indebted I am to you for saving me the loss of that portrait. You may rest quite easy — we are not a bit too kind."

The others, too, had each some cunning word or way which removed from their gifts the feeling of over-condescension. Out of utter good-will, large-hearted Christmas good cheer, and an unaffected sense of gratitude, they seemed offered. Just as simply Rite took them, enjoyed them so thoroughly as to delight the good hearts of the givers, and felt her pleasure doubled in the thought of the comfort the folks at home would take in them. This is another of the ways in which I mean that Rite was rich. She knew how to multiply all her pleasures by *somebody else*, and that made them so much bigger.

This doubling and trebling of enjoyments is a valuable secret. Try it.

Lynde came to see her on Christmas Day, of course. Somebody came every day from home. He brought her the simple book-rack which he had carved for her, by the aid of the Genii, and told how the others were saving up their presents for her until she could come home. They were all small things, yet, to Rite, so exquisite was . the sweetness of these little home gifts, planned with such patient pains-taking, hoarded with such care, and given with such love, that no costlier presents, of less familiar hands, could crowd them from their first place in her heart. In Lynde's boyish thanks, and in mother's mother-note about the Christmas drawer where Rite last night had bade her look, she quite lost, too, any sore-heartedness about the larger offerings she had wished she might get for them all.

With her hand under her cheek, and her mother's note pressed close in, and all the day's gifts in her sight, Rite said to herself:

"O, how rich I am!"

And she planned how she would try to help more at home, and learn faster, and love better; how she would sympathize with Lynde, and dress Dolly's old rag babies, and wear the pieced-down merino this winter without minding a bit.

She was well enough to be carefully wrapped up and carried home in season to spend New Year's there. How glad and proud they were to have her back! Everything brightened at her coming. The melodeon was open, and had a new piece of music on it, that Lynde had bought for her at Christmas. Her rosetree had a bud half blown. Dolly's tea-set was set out. All the Christmas tokens she had not seen yet were arranged in the most effective way about her own room. She would not once think how different it was from Maud Sylverner's luxurious, rosy room, in its bare and meagre look. O, no! It was all dear to her, and the holiday trimmings relieved the high, white walls.

She tried the new songs, and played her father's old favorites, answered the anxious questions about the sprain and the burn, and surfeited Dolly with new stories.

Her mother insisted on tucking her carefully in when she went to bed that night, and then sat down on the edge of the bed to hear the last of what Rite was telling her about Miss Maud Sylverner's new dress for a Twelfth Night masquerade to which she had been invited.

"Are you sure you'll be just as contented now, darling?" asked Mrs. Hollis, a little anxiously. "It is so still and lonely in this great, empty house, I know, and you have just seen so much wealth and gaiety."

"Why, yes, mother! more contented than ever!" answered Rite, in a simple, honest way, that satisfied her mother. "Don't you see, I'm so much the richer now? I can shut my eyes any time and go walking with my thoughts all over that beautiful Sylverner house, and take the good of it, just as if it was mine. Why, it's almost having it! And Miss Maud said she should not forget, but surely come to see us. But even if she didn't ever come, I have all my good times to remember!"

However, Miss Maud did come. She liked Rite, nor was it a family to forget the obligation which they owed to Rite for her discovery of the fire. Rite's life, so different from her own, interested Maud, too.

Rite showed her through the spacious, disused house, the carved cornices over the lofty windows dusty, the sculptured urns in the hall-niches discolored, the frescoing faded and dull. The library, opening on the south piazza, among the shrubbery, was blocked up with a stack of furniture, swathed in white.

One naked mirror only occupied the ample drawing-room; parlors and music-room were empty. Rite pushed the creaking, unwilling shutters aside, to show Maud the view, from the up-stairs windows, over the river. She even recounted how she amused herself by making up stories about the tower-room, and the chamber that had belonged, it was said, to a beautiful Miss Guinivere, who died.

"And this is my room," said Rite. "In winter I have the warm south-room; and, in summer, the one that looks out into the pine trees at the north."

"How grand you are to go boarding round so!" said Maud, gaily.

But the room looked very pinched and barren, to her eyes, as she sat down where Rite placed an old-fashioned chair in the sunshine.

The floor was bare, save for a strip of carpet in front of the bed; the pine bureau and claw-footed table, in spite of the taste with which Rite kept all her belongings arrayed upon them, appeared like desert islands in the midst of a great void, to Maud. Only one picture hung on the yellowed walls, so staring and blank. It was the picture of the Christmas Bell, which Maud had playfully given Rite, in its scorched estate, " not to look at, but only to remember the fire by."

" And are you really happy here ? " asked Maud.

" Yes, indeed ! " said Rite, and Maud wondered at the bright, happy face. " For I should be so homesick here ! " thought Maud.

" But when you really love pretty things so much — " began Maud, and then stopped embarrassed; realizing that it was not quite delicate to speak about the lack of these same pretty things.

"Why should one have to *own* pretty things, to enjoy them?" said Rite placidly. "I just enjoy other peoples'. Besides, I've got a good deal of my own. And, anyway — there! That's just it, Miss Maud, I've got my *own!*"

"What do you mean by that? Your own?" asked Maud, not understanding at all.

Rite looked up at the picture of the Christmas Bell, forgetting everything in her earnestness to explain.

"One night," said she, "after I came home from your house, I could not get to sleep, and lay looking at this picture, for mother had left me the lamp. I heard a bell begin to ring somewhere far off; and I began to think over everything I remembered about bells. I wondered how it seemed to the people, when the first bell was heard to ring, away back

in the year 400. I imagined the people putting
out their fires, when the bells rang curfew. The
Philadelphia freedom bell, and the bell that
tolled for little Nell, wedding bells, and fire
bells, and passing bells, mixed themselves up
in my mind. While I was still looking at your
picture, and partly thinking about that, partly
about a question mother had asked me, if I
should be as contented now, a little story came
into my head, that, I thought, would please
mother, and make her sure. Sometimes mother
thinks I don't have good times enough. But
I do! My story went like this : "

Rite looked dreamily out of the window,
as absorbed in her story as if she were
reading it out of a book. Maud listened like
a child, very much interested, too.

" The church bell hung in an ivied tower;
the school bell was shut up in a neat belfry ;
the mill bell's place was ugly and bare.

" The church bell had a great deal to do.
Its duties were solemn and weighty, indeed.

It rang for funeral, and festival, and the services of holy Church.

"Also the school bell worked hard, and though the idle little children dreaded its sound, it really was one of their best friends, and, as such, for years toiled on, ringing punctually, at certain fixed hours on weekdays, and keeping the seventh day.

"But the mill bell's business was to wake sleepy people from their morning naps, and to call the villagers to distasteful loom and spindle.

"The church bell looked down on the school bell; they both looked down on the mill bell, and, indeed, never would join voice with it, except in case of fire. It was vulgar, they said, working only in the sordid cause of dollars and cents. *They* labored for minds and souls.

"Among the villagers, too, everybody would turn to listen when the church bell rang, as to a voice of distinction; everybody respected the school bell; but the poor mill bell received more curses than courtesies. Still it went on about its duty, and made no fuss.

"Now it came Christmas-tide; and now the starlit night before the joyful day; and when the church bell, in its deepest tones, rang out the chimes, the listening people thrilled with pride in the bell, and gladness in its good tidings of great joy.

"But, of a Christmas Eve, when the chimes are ringing, far and wide, through the earth, can't you think that there may be plenty of sights about the world, and above it, that nobody sees? That nobody sees except sometimes an artist, sometimes a poet, sometimes a dreamer, and sometimes a little child.

"And so, on this night, an artist saw in his sleep, just as the chimes began to ring, chains of good sprites and fairies, caressing elves and spirits, floating out upon the sounds and upheld by them. This the artist turned into a picture for everybody to behold.

"But a dreamer saw also, in a vision, like beautiful spirits garlanding and whispering about the common, loud-voiced, work-a-day mill bell.

"'Well done, well done, and faithfully!' they were softly murmuring to the mill bell, 'for it is not the sort but the spirit of the work that tells. Whoever in his own work is faithful, blessed, blessed, be he, this Christmas Eve, of all good spirits!'

"Then the dreamer awoke, and took for his motto these words: 'To every man his work.'

"For when he remembered that the King, who went into a far country, left to every man his work, he wanted to do, *the very piece* which that king had taken pains to pick out for him, alone to toil at. And, though the dreamer is still only a humble worker in the mill, so accepting his work he has a right just as large and sweet as that of any master-hand to the hope of that reward—'Well done, good and faithful servant!'"

"I see just what you mean, now," said Maud gently, as Rite paused.

Maud never pitied Rite again. As she learned to know her, and, as time went on, recognized how the leaven of Rite's sweet, contented spirit leavened the whole clay lump of life, she even came to call her, by contrast to many a fretful, restless rich woman, "The richest girl in town, after all!"

Ah, you see, "Happiness may be of very common materials, the secret lies in the skil which makes them up."

CHAPTER V.

PULLS OUT A PLUM.

CHRISTMAS Eve came round again, and again at twilight the Sylverner house was brightly lit.

Were the guests all there?

Bravely, as they sat around the long, glistening table, was the warm, yellow dining-room tricked out as before with holly and evergreen. The polished oak reflected back the light. The solemn high clock, that carried the moon, ticked just the same in its honored place.

And the Christmas pie furnished royally forth the board. A noble pie, a pretty dish to set before the king! Its ample girth shone like frosted silver in maiden hue of white, its bulging sides were rounded with the same old motto,

"Put in your thumb
Pull out a plum!"

in wonderful inlaid letters of red and gold. Its grand oval top was stuck with colored tapers all a-blaze, and from the unsounded depths came mysterious sounds of music.

Quivers of admiration, rustles of anticipation, went about and about the table round at that goodly sight, yet there was a certain quietness in the elation, which was not there a year ago. How was it, and who was missing?

The host and hostess were in their places. Rodneys and Sylverners, the more remote Swallow cousins from New York, and Periwinkle cousins from the country, had not failed to come. If anything, those girls were prettier than ever. Certainly cousin Red looked as red as ever, nay redder; but no wonder, for uncle Brederode never used to look at her like this, his eyes continually returning to her face.

Rite Hollis was there, with her father and mother, and the sophomore took great pains to be polite to her, evidently.

Like "the flowers that grow between," the children were scattered among their elders; and Ronald was teased with various whispers of, "Hullo, Jack Horner!"

"Hullo, yourself, Thumb!" he retorted, knowing that none of the boys had been backward about putting a thumb into that famous Christmas pie of a year back.

But when Dolly, half shyly, took her turn at the mischief, the little gallant appeared to enjoy the chance of replying, tenderly, "Hullo, Plum!"

The childrens' " Miss Maudie," sitting opposite her "particular friend," changed color every
time she caught his eye, but somehow she
took great pains not to do it; and there
was a sort of uneasiness in her manner, as
she tried to make very merry with the pretty
bride sitting next her.

The baby's mother was beside her husband;
but her face was saddened, and her dress was
changed to black. Is it the beautiful baby
who is missing, then?

Yes, the baby is indeed gone, but nobody
need cry about her. The baby's mother says
so herself, and smiles even while her tears
fall over the tiny Periwinkle who is the
smallest family baby now, and asleep up-stairs
at this minute. The dear little baby was
having a better Christmas than any of them,
they well knew; and the baby's mother said
that she hoped it wasn't wicked to feel easier
about the baby since — since grandma went
to heaven too !

Ah! grandma's chair was empty.

Opposite the high chair, with a white little wreath hung in it, that chair of grandma's, just where it used to stand, was heavily wreathed, and bore one white lily at the top.

If there had been a silence as they took their places; if, in that silence, they could not help the dropping of some tears, it was a happy Christmas still; and neither grandma nor the baby seemed as far off as they had at some other times. They knew that the story which grandma had dictated, and Maud had written out, lay waiting among all the plums in cousin Red's queerest of Christmas Pies.

They knew that grandma had especially left word to have it so, and for them to be merry just the same as though she were there with them. .

" To please me, children." That was what she had said.

So Mr. Sylverner said, in a rather low voice, just before the hush became too painful, "Well, who is to pull out the first plum?"

In a twinkling, cousin Red whisked off the cover with a grand flourish, and behold! As thus the pie was opened, the hidden music-box changed its tune to a lively, familiar air. Cousin Red's voice chimed in with it, Maud's followed, and the sophomore struck in, till, quickly taking the infection, a score of voices round the table were ringing out merrily:

> " Little Jack Horner
> Sat in the corner,
> Eating Christmas Pie ;
> He put in his thumb,
> And pulled out a plum,
> And cried, ' What a great boy am I.' "

The rollicking chorus broke in a gust of laughter that brought the very servants to peep in at the doors. With such jollity opened the Christmas Pie.

"And now fall to, fall to, good hungry neighbors, all!" cried cousin Red's ringing voice, the real holly color brightening in her face, and the twinkles in her eyes glistening like those you see in summer's sunshine on the lake. "Each in his turn put in a thumb!"

"No, no," interposed the host, putting on a grave face; "in old times it was the cook's business to taste the king's dishes first, that he might prove he had mixed no poison therein."

"Very well, very well," rejoined cousin Red, "then I consent to first peril *my* precious thumb."

With prodigious show of smacking lips, of tremendous caution, and vast importance, cousin Red pulled out between thumb and fore-finger a roll that lay on the top. It was sealed with a mighty seal. Carefully breaking this, she plunged into the reading of it aloud, acting well her part of Jack Horner, at that point of his history when he cried "What a great boy am I!" — by an appearance of infinite zest and relish.

The sheets were illustrated, and, as she finished reading, she passed them right and left with a parenthetical, "Have a bit of my plum?" which set the children off into choking fits of laughter.

CHAPTER VI.

PLUM THE FIRST.

ONCE there was a man who wanted to set a quantity of things to rights.

You wonder what things?

To begin with, he thought it was a mistake that he ever turned school-master. He *knew* it was a mistake, that school-teachers boarded round. You see, he had just reached Mrs. Slapjack's in turn, and she had given him cold boiled pork and cabbage, saleratus biscuit, and hot mince pie for supper.

And he had the toothache. Toothache ought

never to have been allowed, he was very sure of that.

Was that all he would have altered if he could ?

O, no! not half.

Mrs. Slapjack and her children, big and little, had all gone to bed. The school-master had explained that he had letters to write, which would keep him up; and Mrs. Slapjack had left him the peppermint bottle. She was very sorry, but she was out of ginger, and couldn't make a poultice.

The school-master plied the peppermint, piled on more wood, and then, instead of writing, bit his pen-handle, and talked to himself :

"I wish I had the power to take in the world to mend. Wouldn't I like to go round like an umbrella-man, and tinker it up!

"It's all out of gear. Now, with just a little nail here, just a drop of oil there, just a crook straightened out, or a screw put in, ' everything could be made entirely different.

"The rich shouldn't be so rich, and the poor shouldn't be so poor. The committee-man shouldn't wear false teeth. The minister shouldn't be so afraid that Christmas-keeping is popery. Uncle Briar should, somehow, have a drop of milk o' human kindness infused into him. Mr. Heather should lose his memory, and then his quarrels with uncle Briar would no longer separate my dear girl and me.

" Dear mother could have me back. Bess could come home from her governessing. I'd set up in business. Machinery is my vocation, after all. We'd buy the old house back, where father used to live; it's going to rack and ruin. Another thing that ought to be stopped — nobody should ever mention the poor-house to poor little Kit and Cat again. And every soul in that dreary poor-house should have such a Christmas dinner, too!

" *O!* " here cried the ambitious school-mas-ter, with a groan. "Hurrah, old Double

Tooth!" and he proceeded to sketch a frantic-looking picture on his sheet of blank papei. The double-tooth was represented as hopping along at a miraculous pace, on long, slender, crooked legs, which it appeared to possess by the dozen, while a peppermint bottle, crawling slowly up on a snail's back, followed in pursuit. Tears were supposed to be running down the peppermint bottle's flat sides, and it leaned from the snail's back at a dangerous angle, as if about to fall backward with exhaustion.

Having completed this rough sketch, the school-master turned over a page, and began to write thus:

"MY DEAR NELL: I am greatly disturbed by the waste and the racket of the conflict at present going on, as faintly portrayed above. Nor am I capable of caring much what sort of stuff I write, under the circumstances. But you said you would not forgive me if I failed to send you a letter before Christmas, with full answers to your questions; and already 'tis the week before Christmas,

> "'And all through the house,
> Not a creature is stirring,
> Not even a mouse.'"

(Here a demure young rat puts its head out from a crack in the door of the corner closet where the cheese was, and winked sarcastically; but, bless you! that deluded school-master was innocently blind to it.)

"Dear Nell! If I only could snatch you away from 'the Skinnings', where the boys stick pins into your chair, and the girls make fun of your back hair.

"Poor mother, too, at the boarding-house; skinching herself, and being jewed by Mrs. Screwe, and all the while worrying her heart out about you and me.

"Yes, I did hint at a certain plan of mine to have you both here with me. You see, the committee-man wanted a music-teacher for his daughter Persis; and I thought, if I could get the place for you, and then find some extra work myself, we could manage all to live together, and have some sort of a home once more. But, ah! as ill-luck would have it, when the committee-man came into school last, he tried to address the children with his new set of false teeth in, that I suppose Persis teased him into getting. Now they are so loose that they will keep slipping up and down; and after I had struggled to keep grave, while watching his ghastly efforts, till I could ill bear more, the slippery things flew out and lit on the edge of the desk, grinning maliciously. The children roared, and I laughed out. Yes, Nell, I confess it—I laughed. The committee-man turned on me a look of unspeakable rage, seized his teeth, and left abruptly. Since which time he will not even look at me in the street.

"Moreover, Nell, I feel—I'm afraid I feel—

as though I'd adopted two children. Don't scold, Nell, you couldn't have helped it yourself. Kate and Christopher Kearney, brightest little scholars in my school last term.

"Their mother was a foreigner by birth — friendless — a widow. Some called her proud, some called her shy, but nobody seemed really to know her. She died suddenly, and when she found herself going, she sent for me, and gasped in such a pitiful, appealing way: 'You — the children — promise! Their only friend — you!' Now Nell, *could* you have helped it? And could you send poor little Kit and Cat to the poor-house, as everybody about here advises me to do? I can't make up my mind to that, and, meanwhile, they're staying at the parson's.

"Good man, the parson, but queer. Does not like to have me make a good time for the school-children Christmas night, with green wreaths, etc., as we used to at home. Molasses is cheap; I meant to have the school-room trimmed up, and give a grand candy boil there, but I can't go against the parson.

"And, O, my unlucky tongue! I went and hinted at it among the children, too, thinking to give them something pleasant to look forward to. How am I to get out of this scrape?

"I am hardly able to answer all your questions about Mary. I only see the dear girl at church; her father forbids me the house, and guards her zealously. She looks, to me, paler and paler every Sunday. I cannot understand why uncle Briar seems to have had for years such an unreasonable hatred for Mr. Heather.

"When I remember the insults and injuries he has perseveringly heaped upon the man he chooses to call his enemy, I almost pardon Mr. Heather for including our whole family in his wrath against uncle Briar.

Stiff, stingy old uncle Briar! how happy he could make us all! I don't want his money, and shall support myself; but if the forlorn

old man, living solitary in his lonesome, shut-
up house, nursing bitter spites, hoarding dollars, alienated from his own sister, our mother,
because her husband died poor and in his
debt, could be made to see—"

"Why, nothing easier!" cried a voice in
the school-master's ear, so abruptly and so
briskly that he let his pen drop. Instantly,
and without in the least wondering at it, the
school-master found his mind taken possession
of by a most brilliant idea. He saw a delicate and effectual means by which to commu-
nicate to all these different people a sense of
their need of being mended in those points
he had just considered. And it seemed the
most obvious means in the world.

Just for one night to rob the General
Delivery Dream Office; this was the grand and
desperate scheme which the school-master had
in his head. There was no trouble about it.
In a moment the wings of a wish—such a

delightful mode of travelling, no noise, no dust, no jolting — wafted him away to an airy building which showed but dimly in the dark, and was open on all sides.

High up appeared the words, shaped in postage stamps piled up like blocks :

DREAMS.
GENERAL DELIVERY OFFICE.

The school-master found himself in the midst of such bustle and business that nobody had time so much as to notice him.

There were real Air Line railroads at that office. Bubbles came floating in continually, linked together in long trains, from north, south, east and west. " Grand Through Route," was inscribed on some of these trains, in beautifully illuminated letters; " Air Line " on others. Immediately upon reaching their destination, each separate car, or bubble, magically collapsed; and down tumbled load after load of

the freight with which they were stored —
which was dreams! I do assure you, nothing
but dreams. Dozens of officials then began
in an orderly manner to sort and distribute
the cargo; while the trains remained slowly
making up again, bubble linked to bubble,
out of the enveloping clouds of fragrant,
floating steam.

Whence the dreams came, the school-master,
in spite of his drilling in geography, could
not always determine. Some of them certainly
bore a familiar, homelike stamp and post-mark.
But many were labelled in a foreign language,
a language utterly unintelligible and unknown
to ordinary men; nobody could trace their
origin.

Most mysterious packets were there, of all
sizes, sorts, colors and shapes; indeed, everything odd seemed represented. The duty of
one official, evidently, was to call a sort of
roll, as he tidily and swiftly sorted the miscel-
laneous piles, and he went on in this manner·

"Hum! allspice. Ha! rose-leaves. Ho! pepper. Ninety-nine wasps' stings. One elephant's eye-lash. Saw-dust. Fog. Bo Peep's lost sheeps' tails. (This seemed to be back hair.) Cobwebs. Kicks. Kisses. Headache. Roasted tack-hammer with sauce. Pickled numerator. Improper fractions — st!" ejaculated the official abruptly, and a policeman, at the sign, confiscated the objectionable packet, while the school-master looked on approvingly, murmuring to himself with a feeling of virtuous satisfaction, "Improper! Of course. The only way." To many more items did the school-master listen with perfect gravity. Nothing was too remote, nothing too ridiculous to be enumerated. As to the addresses, they were to every name under heaven. Great and famous names were there. Poets' names were there, but the school-master, even then, would not have meddled with poets' dreams; who knows what may come of them? Mary Heather's name was there, and the school-master longed to get hold of this one, for would he not have put the picture of himself in ? The dear little Kit and Cat dreams looked so funny and rosy and dainty, like broken bits of clouds left over from making sunset with, that the school-master was sure he could not make them any prettier if he tried.

" But O ! the committee-man's dream ! I must secure that !" mused the school-master eagerly, when he spied it. "Nobody could mix that dream so well as I ! And to Nell I would send a dream all violets and sugar-plums — she gets few enough now-a-days, poor dear ! And Mrs. Slapjack, yeast-cakes, of course; it's a mistake to send her all salera-tus as they seem to.

"And a pinch, right hot out of the oven, for that saucy boy of hers who won't mind."

Here he paused to watch the dream dis-tributors lading and sending off trusty mes-sengers with the sorted and catalogued dreams. These messengers were also very various

There were many thin, lean, quick mosquitoes, fat June bugs, millers in gray uniform, wise-looking night-birds. Fire-fly, more thoughtful than the rest, brought his night-lantern under his flapping cape.

Fairy folks came likewise to help with the mail; in contrast to them, there were a few sinister-looking bats in black dress coats. After all these had been duly laden and sent, the whole force of officials began to pack dreams into the trains which stood ready to run down the golden railways of star-beams and moon-beams, by which direct communication was had with innumerable chamber-windows, and the pillows near them.

For the first time, the school-master then discovered that there is a great difference in pillows. Of course they should all have been so soft that not the most fragile dream dropped there need be shattered — what else are pillows for?

But this did not prove to be always the case,

and some that looked plumpest were so deceitfully hard that several choice dreams were shivered to atoms, and the sleeper tossed uneasily, complaining in his sleep, and even cutting himself with the sharp-edged fragments of the dream left under his unconscious head.

The school-master smiled, in spite of its being no laughing matter, at finding that some pillows were stuffed with squirming, scratching mice, which made it impossible to trust any but very tough dreams there. Some pillows had machinery in them, which frightened the dream-bringers away with their noise. Others were stuffed with gold and silver, by many supposed to be most conducive to ease; but in the present instances far otherwise, as the school-master noted.

But what was his surprise to see his mother's pillow the very stony one that Jacob the Patriarch of old slept on, one memorable night. "I knew we were poor, but has it come to this, that my mother has been obliged to borrow his pillow?" thought the school-master, in dismay at such poverty. Just then through a crack in the stone he caught a glimpse of heart's-ease, and felt comforted. "It must be her own, after all," he reasoned, "for there is nothing said about heart's-ease in Genesis."

While the school-master, not yet decided how to manage the bold deed which he meditated, looked on, his eye fell on one distorted packet which instinct assured him was meant for uncle Briar.

"It will never do to miss this chance!" thought he. His heart beat fast. With one quick motion he smothered the official in charge, under his big black hat, and snatched up hurriedly all the dream-mail matter within reach, in that same instant. He did not stop for breath till he had stowed himself safe away in the school-house, and there examined his pelf. Joyfully he discovered Mr. Heather's name, and the parson's, as well as uncle Briar's. In eager haste the school-master first locked up his prize in the ricketty desk, then hurried to Mrs. Slapjack's and back.

"Pepper, of course," muttered he, fumbling over uncle Briar's packet, and sprinkling in liberally out of Mrs. Slapjack's pepper-box.

Then he bethought himself that, after all, he pitied uncle Briar.

"And it's Christmas time, too," said he; "for that sake I'll put in the drop o' milk of human kindness that I was near forgetting."

Next came the parson's packet, and, not hesitating a minute, the school-master sprinkled in salt, and sealed it up again.

Then he looked over the rest of his handful, and found none addressed to names he knew, save one to the committee-man.

That he laid by itself, to carefully consider over, and because the spirit of pure mischief had entered into him, I suppose; though he would not for a moment descend to the

meanness of opening and reading other people's
letters, he just scattered in, indiscriminately, here
a pinch of mustard, there a trifle of cinnamon,
a pill he happened to have in his pocket, the
fish-hook he had taken from Johnnie Smith in
school-time yesterday, a sum in square root, a
sliver from the North Pole, and all the parts
of speech.

Last he concocted a mixture for the committee-man. It seemed to him a triumph of
ingenuity, and just the thing the committee-
man needed.

But now, how was he to return the pur-
loined missives to the properly-commissioned
mail-carriers, by whom alone these important
dreams could reach their respective destina-
tions? Emboldened by his success, the school-
master returned hurriedly to the spot whence
he had taken the dreams, slipped his budget
slyly under the nose of a busy official, and
conveyed himself swiftly, and, as he supposed,
unobserved, to his chair at Mrs. Slapjack's.

But justice will not be cheated, however a culprit may flatter himself for a while.

The officers of the dream department were on his track; in half an hour that guilty school-master was silently but forcibly ejected from his chair, harnessed into chains that fastened by keys, and found himself being driven at headlong speed by a bumble-bee, to deliver the belated dreams which he had abstracted. Sharply the brisk bumble-bee driver plied his whip, the active sting, over the school-master's shrinking head.

"Spare him not!" had been the order from head-quarters; and panting, stumbling, galloping up hill and down dale, over fences and through floods, the luckless school-master was scourged on by his relentless and never-satisfied driver.

And now the strange team drew up abruptly, and for an instant the unwilling steed, ready to drop, took breath, as the alert bumble-bee, in his unruffled velvet trousers and yellow vest, deftly insinuated the appointed dream through a broken pane of the committee-man's window. In a breath they were off again; but, though he was raced on as madly as before, the school-master seemed now to be strangely absorbed in mind, so that he scarcely noted the road he went. He was somehow made to undergo himself, in a most mysterious manner, all the chances and changes of the committee-man's dream.

It seemed that the committee-man supposed himself to be driving a drove of sheep, only that really they were a set of jumping tooth-aches. That at last, after infinite toil and pains, he succeeded in marshalling them into the school-house. He then called up the first class in ginger, and the second class in mus-tard. To every scholar in these classes who recited correctly, he gave a sound tooth; to every scholar who failed he presented an aching and decayed tooth; from the dunces, he extracted a tooth each for every failure.

A set of false teeth was held up as the prize
toward which the emulation of the whole
school should be directed. Examination day
came, and, just as the visitors assembled, the
committee-man found, to his dismay, that he
had left his false teeth at home by mistake,
and could not speak in any but a foreign
tongue. One of the visitors, with the features
of the school-master, laughed out. "At him!
At him!" cried the angry committee-man, in
plain enough English. Immediately the school,
one and all, flew at the school-master, gnash-
ing on him with their teeth, and leaving him
for dead. But the committee-man was stopped
short in his exultation at this victory, for he
felt a sharp, gnawing pain tearing at his
vitals. He knew that it was the tooth of remorse, and he knew also that it was henceforth his doom to be forever at its mercy.

"Such is the fate of those whom passion and
unforgiving hate carry away!" pronounced the
grave voice of the parson.

Upon these words of wisdom the school-master could not pause to ponder, for presto! it was uncle Briar's dream he must share. Uncle Briar was smarting all over from a severe scourging which avenging imps had administered, while other imps threw pepper on the scars. They bitterly upbraided him because he robbed the world by squeezing thousands out of it, and never giving back a cent's worth of help himself if he could avoid it. Suddenly Nell appeared with a kiss in a pair of candle-snuffers, which she tossed to the suffering man. "It's mother's kiss!" cried uncle Briar; "it's the kiss she gave me when I let my sister have half the apple. She said, I remember, ' *It is more blessed* ' — there! how near I was to forgetting that! But I'll make it up — 'll give my sister her half yet." Muttering to himself, uncle Briar picked half burnt dollars out of the pepper and threw them to Nell. By so doing, he gave the elves such a pelting, that shortly he was left unmolested.

The school-master sobbed with a naughty child, who dreamed of stockings filled with spanks and sticks, and smiled with a good child, dreaming of living with the Swiss Family Robinson in a cave whose walls were of honey and whose posts and timbers were stick candy.

Dreams are sent without respect of persons. That night, at the poor-house, a baby dreamed of an angel, and half-witted Tim thought himself the honored guest of a brilliant wedding feast. When Mr. Heather opened his dream, he was no longer the widowed father, guarding jealously his only daughter, in a stern wilfulness of his own, but was himself a suitor, doubting, striving, hoping, succeeding at last; while Briar Wolcott, rejected for his sake, scowled vengeance, which his happy heart had little heeded then. "Nothing, ah! nothing, should be allowed to thwart true love!" mused Mr. Heather, in his dream. And the school-master's pulses thumped.

But the merciless bumble-bee urged his fail-
ing feet on, to leave the pink dreams for
Kit and Cat, and the parson's dream-mail.
Now the parson was old; but, in his dream,
he was again a boy, hard-worked and under-
fed, saying over to himself ruefully, the old
rhyme about

"'All work and no play.'"

Then he seemed a man again, taking care
of uncounted children. He heard a voice
saying: "Feed my lambs." So he gave the
children plenty of tough bones and hard
crusts, without any salt, and without any
blackberry jam, and wondered that they did
not relish the food. "Feed my lambs," said
the voice again; this time very sadly.

"They are so unreasonable," complained the
parson.

"When I was a child, I thought as a child,
I spake as a child, I understood as a child,"

answered a deep voice. And the parson bowed, silent and rebuked, before a figure of grand, benignant aspect, whom he knew by those words for one of his most revered teachers.

"This is not full tale; more dreams were here," suddenly buzzed the bumble-bee postman, in a voice like a bass drum. "Miserable robber, have you lost them? Yes, yes, without doubt you let them slip from the string, when you went to return the packet." And, by his peculiar, new faculties, the school-master became aware that such had really been the case, and that the stray dreams would never get to their right owners. A dog had picked up one, and was the laughter of his acquaintances, when, in consequence, he barked and whimpered in his sleep. A cat, too, mewed piteously on the hearth-rug, because she had gobbled down too big a dream, and it disagreed with her. A bird was heard to sing out clear and loud at midnight, by mistake. Several innocent people dreamed of the gallows, and some evil ones of the rewards of paradise. All these small irregularities were caused by the miscarriage of the dream-mail, of course.

Whiz, whiz, whiz, went the sting, as the bumble-bee, infuriated, plied it over the luckless school-master. But, with a great cry, the victim, goaded beyond endurance, suddenly awoke.

His watch had stopped, the fire was out, he had tipped the candle-stick over, and it had rolled on the floor. Then the mouse, creeping dauntlessly out, had made such a meal on the candle, as I sincerely hope, to the warning of all gluttons — for he had had enough of the cheese before that — gave him a fearful, if not fatal stomach-ache next day. As to the aching tooth, it was far, far beyond reach of the peppermint bottle, having gained very much the advantage; and, in the early morning, the school-master was seen walking rapidly towards the village doctor's house, with a grim and ferocious aspect.

"What did you get when you opened your
—I mean, what did you dream last night?"
asked the school-master next morning, when,
as usual, Kit and Cat came running out, and
walked to school with him.

"O! angels and mothers and kittens and
Christmas," said little Kit, promptly.

"And you, and candy, and a sled," added
Cat.

Sometimes things more wonderful than
dreams really do come to pass. Things more
wonderful than dreams came to pass before
that Christmas night.

In the first place, uncle Briar had a bad
fall, and was discovered groaning in his barn,
with a broken leg. He was a hard man,
with nobody to tend him for love; and his
nephew went, from pity, to help him, looking
compassionately at the face all written with
crooked lines of avarice, and the cramped,
cunning mouth, now white and drawn with
suffering. He felt the firm screw of necessity

now, and it forced him to say: "Nevvy, send for your mother and Nell, and tell 'em if they'll take care of me, they may have everything their own way, and whatever they've a mind ter ask.

"Oh! this pain's dreadful! Send for 'em, I say! I can't lie here alone."

Now the school-master's sister Nell was a beautiful, bright girl, and both she and her mother had warm, tender hearts to pity and forgive. So the sick old man, who never was well again, received such care and patience that he thawed in spite of himself, and actually had the unaccustomed feeling of being happy. It fell out something like the case in Mother Goose — "The water began to quench the fire, the fire began to burn the stick, the stick began to beat the kid, the kid began to go."

Something — was it the dream? — softened Mr. Heather's heart towards uncle Briar in his adversity. He went to see him on Christmas

Day; he promised pretty Nell to bring his daughter to the school-master's Christmas-night feast for his pupils, which, he said, the parson had spoken to him about.

Indeed, the parson had spoken of it to several people, and kindly, too. Little Kit and Cat's prattling had won him over to the Christmas-keeping. They recalled to his mind the tiny children he had buried years ago.

Altogether, if the school-master was not a happy man that Christmas evening, there never was such a thing in being.

He had no desire to take in the world to mend. He believed as firmly as the parson that the world will all come right, without any of our tinkering.

The committee-man was present at the homely festival, having first sent a great basket of apples. It is suspected that his daughter coaxed him over; or, it may be, that the parson's Sunday morning sermon had made him glad to get rid of resentment, that miserable, gnawing tooth.

Many a more elegant festivity has lacked the heartsomeness of that Christmas evening in the old school-house. There was singing, there was a short speech or two, there was a candy-pull; and, after it was ended, the school-master walked home with Mary Heather, and things were said between them, which — I mean something was decided that — well, never mind! only don't tell the school-master that anybody else ever had a Christmas to compare with that one!

As to Kit and Cat — you may be sure they never went to the poor-house.

Of course, there had to be a merry tumult around the table, as the reading of this story ended. To whom its history belonged was easily discovered, and uncle Buttonover was overpowered with congratulations, as his artist daughter was with compliments.

But the first plum had so manifestly quick-ened all appetites, that the favored tasters

were too impatient for more, long to linger
over the initiatory mouthful.

There was no question now, as to the
individual who should next put in his thumb;
but, with laughing emulation, all the guests
made a simultaneous dive at the Pie; and,
when in a trice it was empty, sank back in
their seats breathless, he who had failed to
secure a plum envying his neighbor, who had
been more successful.

Rite had a plum, but it was the attentive
sophomore who had manœuvred to bring it
about. She would not have been so fortunate
otherwise.

Cousin Red whispered to her, and Rite,
blushing, unfolded rather tremulously the neat
packet, tied with white ribbons, and began to
read in a timid, reverent voice.

Through the written words, grandma's children seemed again to hear the sound of her
vanished voice.

CHAPTER VII.

PLUM THE SECOND.

GRANDMA isn't much of a hand for such things, and, indeed, it would be a queer idea for grandma to take to writing stories at her time of life. But, for all that, I wouldn't miss having a finger in the Pie. So you must let me tell you all, as plain as I can, the memories I have in my mind, just as they come up. I hope the children will understand; I always did like to tell them stories, you know.

When Ronald asked me last Christmas

evening if it wasn't the best Christmas I ever heard of, it was not strange, that, all of a sudden, the Christmas he meant grew to seem farther off and dimmer than some Christmases I spent years ago.

Why, my little grandchildren, I have spent seventy-eight Christmases, and some of you cannot count as far as that.

You know that when I was a child, people did not mind so much about keeping Christmas as they do now. Many, indeed, thought it a really wicked thing to do; and, if it had not been my birthday-time, I should not have had so many pleasant things happen to me then, as I did have. A Christmas present of such a birthday was a good deal, to begin with.

Then, I was for many years, till sister Emma was born, the only girl among many boys at home. They loved me dearly because it had happened so, and I loved them back just as hard as I could.

We used to live in a large, low, rambling house, with a gambrel-roof and windows that had been brought from England.

I think the first Christmas Eve I remember was one which fell on a Sunday. Mother gave me a little brown Testament, that had my name on it in gilt letters, and the boys whispered to me, that, if I would be still as a mouse and never breathe one word about their telling on Sunday, they would let me know every boy of 'em had got a present laid up for me, against to-morrow. And so they had, dear hearts!

But I pretended not to know, because it was Sunday, and father would not have presents given on that day.

Besides, it was a very solemn Sunday, and impressed me, child as I was, so that I never forgot it. It was the day when Priest Pollard — we called our minister priest in New England, in those days — preached the first sermon in our new church. We had met in the school-house till now.

I have been in splendid churches since then,
yes, the grandest in our country, but never
with more awe and solemnity than I felt deep
in my heart that Christmas day, when I sat
in that rustic church. How vast and grand
that solemn, shaded room did look to me!
how sacred every small part of it!

Did you ever wonder how the little Israelite
children felt about the Holy of Holies, that
was behind the veil of the Temple?

Do you suppose they ever imagined to themselves all that was hidden there, and wished,
without daring to say so, that they might
creep in and see?

A little child, who had dared to steal into
that holy place, might have felt as I remember I felt then.

There was a great sounding-board over
Priest Pollard's head; all the people sat in
square pews. When the choir began to sing,
we all stood up, and, turning round, faced
the singers.

"Before Jehovah's sacred throne,
    Ye nations bend with solemn joy."

This was the first hymn, and it was so altogether powerful and impressive to me, that I
felt like crying. But then I was diverted by
the look on my father's face; it had such a
shining of gladness to it.

Priest Pollard preached his famous sermon;
it was quite famous then, and I have it yet,
laid up in the yellow box that was my
father's. I remember, even now, a little how
he looked to me, standing up in the high
pulpit, with the satisfied look on his face,
and the silver crown of his white hair.

When we went home, I asked my favorite
brother, whether Parson Pollard had not looked
like one of the "Shining Ones" in the Pilgrim's Progress. But he said: "I'll tell you
what he looked more like, Say."

And then he found the place in Pilgrim's
Progress, and read aloud to me:

"'This was the fashion of it; it had eyes

lifted up to heaven, the best of books in his hand, the law of truth was written upon his lips, the world was behind his back, it stood as if it pleaded with men, and a crown of gold did hang over its head.'"

I remember, from this Christmas Eve on, how my brothers would contrive some surprise or pleasure for my birthday. Sometimes they would persuade mother to let me have little parties; sometimes they would take me long rides to the city. Once father took me himself. We started early in the morning, and were to come back that same night. While my father went about among the different stores on his own business, I was perfectly happy to trot by his side with my hand in his, and I did not think of expecting anything better. So when he took me into a toy-store at last, and said I might choose a birthday present for myself, 1 could scarcely breathe for delight and surprise, or believe that I had heard right.

"Yes, you may choose just what you like best," said my father, smiling at my wonder.

"Really, father? what I like best? something for mother, and something for all the boys?" I cried out. It did not seem to me possible to want anything else so much as I did that, and father laughed outright and let me have my way. He helped me to choose some little gift for each, and crammed his pocket with the packets, my heart all the while so full of joy that I felt like a child in a story-book and couldn't help wondering to myself whether this were really the same little Sabra that had been so naughty as to lose her gingham sunbonnet no longer ago than last summer, and had had to stay after school only day before yesterday.

When the presents were carried home and distributed, they gave so much pleasure that none of us ever after wished to let a Christmas Day go by without an exchange of gifts similar to this first one. For it was Christmas Day before we reached home.

My father's last errand in the city was to pay a visit to an aged, invalid aunt, the aunt for whom I was named.

It began to storm slightly before we reached her house. In a little while the wind rose and blew like a hurricane, drifting the snow as it increased, and seeming to pull and tear at everything like a dog when he has set his teeth in something he is determined to have.

My father was anxious and uneasy, but there was only one thing to do, for we could not drive home in such a storm, and aunt Sabra was very glad to keep us all night.

I wish I could make you see that low, large room, where, after supper we sat together. The logs burned bright in the fire-place, and the warm, red light put the candles to shame as it danced all over the stiff, old-fashioned furniture, the big, polished locker, and the pictures on the walls. I sat on a stool at aunt Sabra's feet very quiet, and very happy,

and she fed me peppermints. I loved
to hear the storm roar; it made me feel
cast-a-way, like Crusoe, only in a perfect paradise of a place. When, in the twilight, I saw
the slender fir-tree, close up to the window,
writhe and bend in the high wind, it made
me sigh with content to think how warm I
was housed, how safe I was, and what treas-
ures I knew of packed away in father's
pockets.

Aunt Sabra even let me have boxes of hers
to look over, and told me stories about the
contents of them. By and by she had apples
brought in, hickory nuts, and delicious seed
cookies and sugar-cakes.

There seemed to be no kind thing she
would leave undone for us.

And aunt Sabra could talk well. My father
lost his anxious look, as he listened to her,
and stopped walking to the window to look
out.

While they were talking about many things

which I could not understand, I left my low seat and went slowly round the room, looking at all the pictures. There were a good many, and nearly all were curious, for the ladies in them carried huge fans or unnatural flowers; the gentlemen appeared in wigs, and the children wore outlandish clothes. One large landscape represented a sort of rural festival, held near a castle. In the castle tower was a real clock; and I was never tired of watching the tiny hands move. But there was one picture that I went back to again and again — the picture of a beautiful lady. I thought I had never seen as beautiful a face, and it fascinated me to have those watching eyes follow me so constantly, as they seemed to do.

When aunt Sabra asked: "Which picture do you like best, child?" not even the cunning clock-picture could win me from my choice of the beautiful lady.

"And I wish the picture was mine, aunt Sabra," I added earnestly, "because I should never dare to do wrong with those eyes looking at me so all the while, to see if I did. I suppose nobody ever does do wrong here."

At this aunt Sabra went away, and when she re-entered the room, with her slow, feeble step, she put into my hands a ring with a yellow stone in it. The yellow stone seemed to shine like a lighted candle, as I turned it to the fire-light. This very ring, aunt Sabra said, had belonged to the beautiful lady of the picture. The stone was a topaz, which is the November stone, and means *fidelity*. Then aunt Sabra told me the story of Agatha Sylverner, whose portrait, painted in her girlhood by a famous artist, was the one which had so taken my fancy. Aunt Sabra told it well. Many a time my father reminded me of it afterwards, and took pains that I should remember it.

One November, now long ago, Agatha Sylverner was born over the seas.

Her home was one of luxury and ease, but

she left it to follow into our new, rough land
the one suitor whom she loved above all.
As the faithful wife of this poor man she
worked hard in the primitive home to which
he brought her. She not only kept the
house and helped to care for the farm, but
by and by held a little school for the in-
struction of her own children and the neighbors' children.

Plainly as she dressed, she always wore
one ornament. It was a ring set with a
topaz stone, and sometimes, when a child in
her school had been very, very good, he took
courage to beg that he might take the
yellow ring and look at it. Inside it were
graven in tiny letters, for a posy — as the
inscription within a ring used to be called —
the words of a Latin motto, which struck
the ignorant little children with superstitious
awe. These words meant, Mistress Agatha
told them:

> " But trust me true,
> It holds me true."

The children thought of the ring as something very precious, but how should they know all it was to Mistress Agatha?

It was an old, old ring, that had been her own mother's. When pretty, proud Agatha fell in love with her distant cousin, Richard, who was poor, but proud, too, and when they both found it out, not until the very day he was to sail away to the new country, seeking his fortune, he said:

"Dearest Mistress Agatha, if I love you I must give you up, for I am poor and humble — I have all to earn. I am going to the new country. I cannot ask you to wait for me here till I come back. Many richer suitors will crowd around you. For your own sake, Mistress Agatha, I must give you up."

But wilful, noble Mistress Agatha replied:

"I shall never give you up, though you do give me up. Go; make a little place big enough for me in the new country, and I

will wait here. I give you my mother's
ring, and if you think of my richer suitors
and doubt me, read the posy in the ring.
When you have made the little place big
enough for me, I promise you that if you
so much as send me this same ring for a
token, I will come to you."

What man could not have worked like a
giant with such inspiration? With speed
Richard made his "little place" for Mistress
Agatha, and then, when he found that he
could not go in person to claim his treasure,
by a trusty ship he sent the ring back
over the ocean, and fearless Mistress Agatha
herself brought it again to him, proven as
true to him as his trust was true to her.

With this ring the two were married, and
busy, honorable lives they must have lived
together for many years.

But one day the husband bade his wife
Agatha good-by, and rode off on horseback
through the woods, charged with important

business, to the largest town in the region.
Days, weeks, months went by, and he never
came riding back.

His wife neither sank under this blow, nor
went wild; only it is said that she changed
from this time. Her hair whitened, she grew
more stately and silent, and she never let
anyone take the yellow ring from her finger
again. Busy as she had always been, she
worked much harder now. Still she carried
on the farm, and trained the children, but
now she seemed also to try to take up all
those duties to the town and state and church
which her husband had borne a faithful part
in. Richard had been counted a shrewd and
prudent adviser, and his mantle seemed to
have fallen on his wife. The neighbors wondered at her good judgment, while, half-unconsciously, they depended on it. The elders in
the church, who would have scorned the idea
of admitting a woman to their councils, nevertheless admitted the force of her opinions.

There were not wanting those who had accused the missing man of wanton desertion; but so intense was his wife's white anger, when this was once whispered to her, that none ever dared speak to her of it a second time, though they said among themselves, "He has gone back to England. He will never come again."

And there were men, who, seeing Mistress Agatha's sagacity and beauty of character, tried to persuade her that her husband was dead, and to press upon her other love and shelter.

Almost fiercely she rejected every such offer; and when once the parson himself tried to intercede for a worthy suitor, she took the ring from her finger, it is said, and read the Latin words aloud.

"He shall know when he comes back," she said, "though others have dared to deem him false, his wife, by the power and evidence of her faith in him, has never, no, never once doubted him, or admitted that he will not return. The ring is his message to me," she said; "night and day it is my comfort, my good company.

"It beats against my finger like his heart, and says, '*But trust me true, It holds me true*,' as he would say. Nay, Parson, I will hear no word more. All things are possible to him that believeth, and I believe."

Abrupt, even stern, as Mistress Agatha was sometimes, wilful and unreasonable as they thought her, the people could not help loving her, for she herself was loving in spite of all, and generous and helpful in their times of trouble.

She was a wonderful nurse, seeming to have exhaustless strength, and, better than all, the healing talent, the insight into disease, which can only come as Nature's special gift. She became famous for miles around, and was reverenced almost like a saint for her cures. Even remote Indians heard of her power to heal, and came long journeys to ask help of her, which she always gave fearlessly. It may be, that, as she went her way to distant sick people, or followed Indian guides to forest camps, she had the constant, wild hope, of discovering some trace of her lost husband.

Returning one night from such an expedition to the camp of a dying chief, she dismissed the surly guide who had accompanied her, and slept heavily.

But with the morning a bitter loss became apparent; the beloved yellow ring was gone from her finger. She immediately divined that the thievish Indian must have stolen it from her while she slept; but despite her usual clear sense, a superstition stole over her mind that it was an ill omen. Her courage so far failed that she yielded to illness, and her old energy did not return to her till a contagious sickness spread through the town about her. Once more rallying at this, she went from house to house, as if unconscious of her own existence in the care for others.

Haggard and tired from watching, she drew

near her own door after a night's suspense
at the bedside of a child whom nothing could
save to his clinging parents; she met at her
very gate a gray-haired, still noble-looking man,
bent, and strangely clad. "The parson told
me," he said with a wandering air, and lift-
ing his thin hand to his head somewhat
feebly.

As he lifted it, something dropped at Mistress Agatha's very feet in the dewy grass,
and with a hungry cry she snatched up the
yellow ring where it had fallen; crying, "I
did, I did trust you true, my love, my
love!"

The night of weeping was over, and joy
had come with the morning.

After they were thus re-united, the husband
and wife seemed to change characters again.
Mistress Agatha became strangely gentle, almost
timid, and the bent figure of her husband
Richard regained a fearless energy. The wife
could scarcely bear to hear all that the husband

had to tell of his capture by a far-off tribe of Indians whose sullen revenge had never forgotten the death of one of their number by the hand of one bearing his name. Their cruelties, and the hopelessness of his struggles to escape, had well-nigh reduced the captive to utter idiocy at last. A strange apathy seized him, and if he thought of home and Agatha, he also thought, "By this time she must have forgotten me, must have made for herself another home, for every one would love her. I may as well die here, for I should be but a ghost to trouble her, even could I return."

From this apathy, as by an electric shock, he was roused by the sight of the yellow ring. The Indian who had stolen the glittering thing dared not return to his own tribe, but joined himself to the more distant one where the captive was forced to toil for his savage masters. Here the thief exhibited the ring as the gift of a wonderful medicine-woman, and declared that it had magic qualities by which she wrought wonderful cures. When the almost despairing prisoner saw it, new life thrilled through the half-palsied brain in its stupor of despair. First a sharp pang stung it into action, with the thought: "Has she lightly parted with our troth-ring?"

And then the tested words of the posy rang over and over in his mind: "*But trust me true, It holds me true;*" and, angrily reproaching himself for even the shade of doubt, manly hope and courage revived. Often as he had failed in efforts to get free, he now believed, that, for his wife's sake, he would succeed. Indeed, he almost believed that she had contrived to send him the ring, and with it the scheme for escape which suggested itself to his quickened fancy. He assumed a mysterious majesty of manner, and, representing to the superstitious Indians that he had been in a trance, where he had learned the charms of healing by which alone the ring could be made of use, as in the hands of the medicine-woman, he obtained the handling of the ring, and a sort of authority in the tribe.

This led the way to added liberty and the chance he sought for flight; and, persevering in it with a confidence and daring that seemed inspired, he had arrived back safe, to reward Mistress Agatha's faith at last.

" Perhaps, nephew, it would be as well if we did believe more in the constraining power of faith over each other," said aunt Sabra dreamily, to my father, as she finished the story.

What my father answered, I do not know; but I remember that he took me in his arms and rocked me, singing sleepy old psalm-tunes, for a long while, before I could cease trembling from the excitement of the story, and get to sleep.

In the morning the fascination of Mistress Agatha's soft, watching eyes was still strong upon me; and aunt Sabra said, as she told me good-by, "Well, little namesake, when I am through with them I promise you that the yellow ring and the portrait you like so much shall be yours."

She did not forget it. They became mine when I was a girl in my teens. They came with us here to the West when we moved. Everything had changed about us in the old place. The railroads, and the mills established farther down in the valley, had left our village idle and empty. The boys were restless; Priest Pollard and many of my father's old friends were dead; and so at last we came to try a new home, and moved here, old clock and all. My father would never part with that.

Out of fairy tales, a city never sprung up quicker than this one has since that night. When we came it was almost all forest still. And yet, to me, that autumn night does not seem longer ago than last week, when we reached at nightfall the house which looked so bare and small to us, though it was the best in the region then. Now a vast marble block stands just where that low, rough house did. Then the black woods cast their shadows round it, for the woods were pushed back only a short distance, as it were at arm's length, from it, and the sun had just set. We felt like actors playing our parts to bare boards; for there was no one to welcome us, and no house in sight. Our covered wagon, and the load of goods behind us, made all the stir there was, and how I did long for an audience!

Instinctively I pressed the topaz ring on my finger; it reminded me to be brave. Ever since the ring had been made mine, I had kept it carefully, never wearing it common, but putting it on when I had special need to be strong and hopeful.

It seemed to me that at such times I did better for having the touch and the sight of brave Mistress Agatha's ring.

I began to laugh and sing a little, and I worked fast and briskly.

In ten minutes we had a roaring fire, and candles lit, and were ·hungrily preparing for supper. But here we found ourselves met by such a calamity as we could hardly credit at first. Fancy our dismay when we began to suspect, that, by some mistake which nobody knew anything about, the great hamper of cooked provisions, and most of our household stores, had been left behind for the next load to bring on to-morrow!

We looked at each other blankly; then everybody fell to searching over all sorts of impossible barrels, boxes and bundles, simply because we felt our situation an incredible one, impossible to accept.

In the midst of it I felt little Eunice pulling at my sleeve. She was little Eunice then, and we called her the baby still.

"Sister Say, are we going to starve?" She looked at me with very sad, solemn, dark eyes as she asked me.

"Why, no; no indeed!" I answered, with my head half-way down a box of bedding.

"Sister Say," I heard her say again, "why don't somebody look down cellar? We could eat potatoes, you know."

At this one of the boys laughed and cried out; "Hear the little wise-pate! She thinks potatoes grow on cellars. Don't you, Eunice?"

"Why, they do at home," said the baby, innocently. She had always been used, you see, to the great, crowded bins and barrels of the cellar at home, which she had always seen full.

I took little notice of the teasing that the boys gave Eunice after that, for I had come upon the portrait of my ancestress, Agatha Sylverner, where I had carefully packed it myself between the blankets. Reaching up I set it squarely on the high mantel shelf, and, with something of my old childish attraction towards those steady eyes, I was standing in a sort of dream looking into them, when I heard the door behind me click.

There was Eunice, half-tumbling up the last cellar stair, her dancing eyes and red cheeks shown by the dripping candle she had in one hand, while the other held up her apron full of something.

" O, I told you so ! I told you so !" she exclaimed, breathlessly: " there *were* potatoes there ! I knew God wouldn't let us starve !" And, tripping in her eagerness, Eunice fell into the room as she spoke. The candle expired and rolled off in company with a quantity of carrots, that had nimbly sprawled out of Eunice's apron. We picked up the child and the carrots, amidst a general shout over "Eunice's potatoes," which father declared would make a capital supper, nevertheless; and, in the midst of our merriment, there was a crash.

We had fairly shaken the unsubstantial walls of our new home in our merriment, and I

sprang to pick up my precious portrait of
Mistress Agatha, which had been thus rudely
dislodged.

There was no injury beyond a slight loosen-
ing from the frame, and I had scarcely begun
to say so when I caught sight of some yellow,
folded papers that had been jarred from their
concealment in the frame by the abrupt fall.

I drew them out tenderly, and hid them in
my bosom, then, when we were quiet again, we
shared them all together, and exulted over
them as in having found great treasure.

For they were love letters; love letters between Mistress Agatha and Richard her
betrothed.

There were only four of them, though many
others may have passed between them that
were lost, for whose hand had hidden these
so deftly we could never know. The words
had been written more than a century ago,
but they seemed as tender, as vivid, and as
fresh as yesterday's flowers. Do you wonder

that no other feast can make me forget the one where the fare was "Eunice's potatoes," eaten so mirthfully, with keen appetite, around the bare but blazing hearth, and where, in-stead of speech or toast we all listened, hushed, afterwards, to hear these old love letters read aloud?

Perhaps none of us young folks who heard these quaint letters read had ever known be-fore what real, pure love is like. Silly young thing that I was, I had myself never known before.

There is no harm in my telling now that I had two suitors in those days.

One could offer me the command of what they called a fortune then, and a home in the old place that I was homesick after. The other, younger, and just beginning life in the new West, where he had come a year or two before us, had said himself, in the letter that had reached me but just before our removal: "I know I can only offer you love. But will you take love?"

Somehow the confusion between these two suitors, which I had been feeling, went quite away as I pored over Mistress Agatha's yellow love letters. I wondered that I could have been confused at all. Words that I had often heard Parson Pollard read, in the high pulpit at home, came back to me with a peculiar authority: "Many waters cannot quench love, neither can floods drown it: if a man would give all the substance of his house for love, it would utterly be contemned."

When my birthday came again, that year my lover spent it with me, the happiest Christmas of my life I thought then, and after a while we were married, your grandfather and I.

We were very fortunate. My father lived to see this house built, and a city growing up around us. Still, we saw some hard times, with our little children and pioneer work. I've often told you stories of it all.

But now everything seems pleasant to remember, taking it all in all, and I have even grown used to thinking of my husband and some of my children, and those I loved best, as safe in Heaven, when the Christmas time, we used to take such pains to keep together, comes round.

And when my children in their turn miss me, I should like them still to keep the dear old festival gladly and with honor.

Rite's voice, which had followed the story with sympathetic tenderness, stopped; and little Dolly was the first to speak, for the elders only looked at each other rather dim-eyed.

"Is that really the lady in the picture?" asked Rite, eagerly.

Maud answered her:

"Yes, that is Mistress Agatha's picture, the one Rite saved from getting burned up, that hangs in the drawing room. And see! this is the topaz ring!"

All the children crowded round Maud to look at the yellow stone in its quaint setting, dull and tarnished now with age. It hung loosely on Maud's slender finger, and the children regarded it full of respect and awe. Then, while Ronald took them away to gaze up into the portrait's wistful eyes with new interest, Maud drew a thin packet of yellow, folded sheets from her pocket.

"Some of you have never seen our precious love letters," she said, and passed them to the bride. "Grandma gave the charge of them and of the ring to me.

"You know I wrote her story out for her, as she told it to me by degrees. She seemed to enjoy every word of it, and was so anxious to have it finished, that it might be ready for the Pie."

Very lovingly they handled the worn letters as they were passed about, speaking to each other softly over them, and not ashamed if a tear dropped now and then on the faded ink, lingering over the words that were made by the power of true love so living and full of sweetness, as if unwilling to turn from their contemplation.

But the children came trooping back and clamored, "More! more! another plum!" — for when were children ever satisfied with stories? "Plum! Plum! who's got the plum?" they began to cry.

The bride tried to look very unconscious as one of the Swallow cousins, at a sign from cousin Red, began to read.

CHAPTER VIII.

PLUM THE THIRD.

THIS story opens in the midst of a merry little quarrel between two people. In the first place, He Says that he means to have his own way about it, and be sure that it is told right. And as she cannot help herself about that, She Says, Very well; there shall be no mistake about it, then; none of his sayings shall be ascribed to her, but shall be carefully set down as what He Says. Therefore, it begins with what

159

SHE SAYS.

She was going into the country for the summer, and was within two or three miles of the place where she was to stop, when the rattling stage drew up. It was a pretty place. The road was curving through a meadowy valley, that looked just right for pitcher-plants and choice wild flowers to grow in. A high ridge of hills sheltered it on one side, and a river wound quietly through it, which had, just here, a rather long, covered bridge over it.

At one side of this covered bridge, there was a watering-trough; and when the young lady passenger found that the stage would stop long enough to water the horses, she sprang out of the stage just to rest herself by the change, and to gather a cluster of wild roses, that looked irresistibly pink and bewitching, against an old stone wall.

"Please will you have a drink of water?"

This timid question met her the moment

she stepped down, aided by a gentleman who politely rose to help her.

A brown, girl-face looked up, shy but eager, with the question; and a very brown little hand held up a clean cup of water. As the young lady looked at the faded, out-grown dress and bare feet of the petitioner, another voice spoke, more fearlessly, but quite respectfully:

"A cup of water, please, ma'am? Or a flower?"

And the boy's cheek flushed as he looked up honestly, while the girl seemed confused at her own daring, and could only stand and stare.

HE SAYS.

It was no wonder. I presume those children had never in all their lives before seen anything so pretty as the young lady was in her travelling-suit. I never had.

SHE SAYS.

While the young lady sipped her cup of water, she looked about her, and saw a pretty sight.

Under the covered bridge, at one side, the children had made a delightful little cubbyhole. They had put up two or three rough shelves, and covered them with lichens and fresh, green mosses. On these shelves they had arrayed, as temptingly as they knew how, their stock in trade — bunches of wild flowers, birch-bark baskets filled with berries, bird's nests and neatly woven wreaths.

In a cool corner beneath, stood the covered pail of pure water; and, with oak-leaf garlands, and boughs of maple and cedar, they had made the whole into a rude bower. The young lady was so pleased with it all, that she gladly paid for the cup of water, and one of the birch-bark baskets besides; then, while she selected some flowers, she asked questions.

HE SAYS.

And managed it very cleverly, too.

SHE SAYS.

She found out that the black-eyed boy and the shy girl lived in the little, old red house that you could see just around the corner, over the bridge. They were orphans; their parents lay in the small, square enclosure right across the street, with its half dozen melancholy white slabs. Their grandmother, who took care of them, let them have this "store," as they called it proudly. She could not spare them to go as far as the school and be gone all day; she was too old and sick now.

But she could spare them to rig up their store and to "keep it open" every day when the stage went by.

"Wouldn't somebody else like to buy?" the boy asked, like a thrifty little tradesman.

His business-like, grave airs amused the

passengers looking out of the stage windows. Some of them good-humoredly bought flowers or baskets; and, as the young lady, having to hurry into the stage again, promised the children to come again, she saw the gentleman, who had helped her out, slip something into the little girl's hand.

HE SAYS.

And what right had she to see anything of the sort? It was all along of that, probably, that she slipped, as she climbed in, and spilt half her berries.

SHE SAYS.

The stage started off briskly, the kind-hearted driver having been slow about watering his horses, on purpose, and having taken a long draught of cold water on his own account. It seems that he knew all about the children.

"Sorry for 'em, sorry for 'em," said he,

when one of the passengers asked some question, "it's a pretty poor sight ahead for 'em,
with nobody belonging to 'em but their old
grandma, and a blind brother, they've got,
that's up to the 'sylum. P'r'aps you'd like to
know what they've got this store of theirn
up for. They think, maybe, they can get
money enough by it, to go and see him, poor
things, there at the 'sylum."

The stage, and all the other passengers,
went rattling out of sight, leaving the young
lady at the gate of a farm-house, whose hospitable tenants came hastening out to welcome
her. It was a farm-house as big as a barn,
with elms in front, cool, quiet; and, to the
young lady's taste, one of the pleasantest
summer places in the whole world. She had
been here before, and knew all the pleasantest
walks and drives.

But there was so little to vary life in that
still farm-house, that there really was no
reason why she should forget the small shop

keepers, who had interested her on the way thither. Besides, whenever you went to the village, where the stores, the churches and the post-office were, you had to cross the bridge. And so, whenever she drove that way, she used to stop and buy and talk; and, by degrees, grew thoroughly acquainted and familiar. It was all true about the children's orphanhood, and the lonely way in which they lived, supported by the scanty sum of money which their father had left at his death.

It was true about the blind brother, who was at the asylum in the city. The village doctor had arranged for his entrance there, when he became blind; and ever since, this younger brother and sister at home had yearned to go and see him.

"O!" said the little sister, "he cried dreadful when he had to go and leave us, and so did we. But me and David we promised him, the very last thing, we'd come and see him, if he had to stay long."

Then the little Rachel told how they had contrived different ways, in the hope of earning money to go with; and that, at last, they had thought of this way.

Because, one day, when they were building a play-house in the covered bridge, as the stage came by — the great event of the day in that out-of-the-way place — a thirsty lady had given them a cent for the loan of a cup to drink water from.

" Then me and David thought," said Rachel, "that maybe other people would like drinks of water, too, or bunches of flowers. And the stage-driver is so kind to us; and we've got quite a heap of pennies now in the old tin tea-pot. I hope it's 'most enough. I know that poor Jasper he expects us."

The grandmother described how her grandson had lost his sight. "He was such a stiddy boy," she said, "only thirteen years old, but so noticin' and handy, and worked in the gardin, most like a man. He was a great hand for flowers and sich. O, deary me! his poor old grandma'am won't ever forgit how o' daisy-time, yes, just daisy-time, arter he'd been a-complainin'-like for some time of things dancin' like flies afore his eyes, Rachel she come and brought him in some daisies, and, says he: 'Yes, I'll look at 'em as long as ever I can; I'll never see 'em again.' And, sure enough, they was the last posies he ever could see, poor boy! or ever will, fuz I know. He was sick arter that, quite a long while, and the doctor was 'mazin' kind.

"He's a good man, Dr. Haddam is. He took all the trouble of gettin' Jasper into the 'sylum, soon's he was able to go. He said he could be helped by the doctors there, if he could at all — still, deary me! I hain't much faith."

But the young lady was hopeful, and tried to make these sad people hopeful, too. She counted the money in the tin tea-pot, and made a grand plan, which put the two chil-

dren in raptures, for taking them with her on
her return to the city, and giving them the
coveted chance to go to the asylum. Her
father, who spent most of the Sundays with
her, at the farm-house, consented quite will-
ingly to this. He was interested himself in
the children, and always bought at the Covered Bridge establishment.

HE SAYS.

I have since been credibly informed, that
she herself was perfectly reckless in her
extravagant purchases all summer; also, that
the extent to which she made up calico, and
made over delaine for Rachel, and hunted up
clothes for David, was enough to ruin any
father's patience but her father's, when one
considers that he had sent her into the country to rest. It has even been said, that she
actually helped the children to arrange their
ingenious store in the covered bridge, sometimes. There is no doubt that she taught

them speller and reader; and, as to Sunday-school — ·

SHE SAYS.

Really lovely things went on sale at that rustic store. It was as if the whole year passed in procession through it. Flowers, of course, they had, all the summer through, from early arbutus and violets to late gentians; every sort of berry, sassafras roots, herbs, wild grapes; and, from their garden, caraway and dill. They became really skilled and tasteful in arranging their wares, and learned to make graceful rustic contrivances for baskets, easels, photograph frames and brackets, out of the abundant material supplied by the woods. Their friend, the young lady, was amusing herself by making a large fernery, and they had a standing order from her, for all the choice ferns and mosses, pitcher-plants and vine-roots they might succeed in finding. When it grew colder and later in the year, still the persevering children offered their autumn leaves, grasses, bitter-sweet and red alder berries, which summer visitors, leaving the country, often bought gladly. It was quite touching to see how staunch and brave they were for Jasper's sake, never missing a day in rain or heat, wind or snow, but always keeping at their post, when the stage passed by.

November was near, however, and the children looked rather sad as they saw how soon they must close the business up.

HE SAYS.

And once, when they were almost crying over their empty shelves, on the day of an early snow, what do you suppose she coaxed the farmer's wife into letting her have?

A big panful of doughnuts, to be sure, and then went herself and made coffee.

The children found the hearty fare so well relished by the people in the stage that they made nearly two dollars by it.

David always affirmed that the stage-driver ate himself six doughnuts on the spot, and carried away a dozen more.

SHE SAYS.

However, the time drew near when the grand end of their toils was to be reached, and the young lady was to take them with her to the city. It was really quite a nest-egg that had gathered in the tin tea-pot, and with part of the little fund a woman was found to stay with grandmother Conway while they were gone.

At last they stood one morning, dressed in their modest best, and full of excitement, waiting for the stage to come along and take them in.

How happy they looked when the driver reined up and winked at them, and their young lady put her head out to nod very reassuringly at proud but trembling grand- mother. It was a great day to them all.

Rachel, sitting close to her friend, whispered:

"I am carrying a few things out of the woods to Jasper. But if I only had some flowers, he liked them so much! If I could only find a daisy! Because, perhaps, we shall find him so much better that he could see one again.

"You remember what grandmother tells about his saying when he was getting blind? And I want to have a daisy for him to see the first thing, if he does get well again, shouldn't you?"

It would be nice, the young lady said, but, of course, it was too late for daisies now; even the gentians were gone; and Rachel's brother would be sure to like any of the out-door things that came from home, she thought.

After this was it not like a story-book — but it really happened; indeed, no story-book can be so wonderful as things that happen in life — that Rachel's eye, on that bleak morning,

should catch, about half way between the bridge
and the village, where they were to take the
cars, the sight of a single patch of daisies,
nodding in the chill breeze, large and serene
as ever, and evidently not at all aware that
their white and gold looked as out of season
as a last summer's dress.

Rachel clapped her hands with a cry of
delight that made everybody start; she called
to the driver in a tone so shrill that he
stopped the horses before he knew what was
the matter.

In half a minute Rachel, followed by her
brother, had picked a handful and they were
back in the stage again. Nobody grumbled,
least of all the driver, it had happened so
quickly, so spontaneously. The daisies brightened the stage, full of shivering people, who
looked at them wondering and smiling. The
dear little fear-naughts !

We all know they are of the hardiest,
most cheerful stock in all Nature, with the

open, clean, honest face, and the bright up-
look at everybody, but they are not apt
to bloom, among mountain regions, as boun-
tifully and fearlessly as these did in mid-
autumn.

The driver himself, knowing all about Rachel
and the blind boy, touched them tenderly
with his large, rough hand, as he helped
Rachel down. Perhaps it was foolish of
Rachel's friend, but it did seem to her like
a good sign sent on purpose.

With looks of perfect content Rachel hugged
her bunch of daisies during the long car-
ride, letting them lap lovingly against her
crimsoned cheek, and many a stranger looked
curiously at them.

One lady in mourning begged, "Could the
little girl spare her just one?" And when
she left the car, she put something into Rachel's
hand as she passed her — a silver coin that
had a hole in it.

Rachel and David felt very subdued in the

strange, loud city. It was not hard to make it very entertaining for them, and their young hostess, who was an only child, found the care of them a pleasing novelty. So, though it was a great disappointment to find that they could not see their brother at once, yet their thoughts were constantly diverted, and all the while, without being conscious of it, they were learning much from all they saw and heard. Nor did they fully understand, as their friends did, through what a critical time their brother was passing.

When it had first been decided that he could regain his sight only through a delicate and critical operation, the doctor had found him too weak in health and reduced in strength to endure it at once. So that during the months past they had been carefully nursing and bracing him, and, when Rachel and David came, had but just accomplished the final operation. Its success depended afterwards upon perfect quiet for some days in a darkened room, with bandaged eyes. Little Rachel, who could not understand why they would not let her go to her brother, begged, with tears, that at least she might send her daisies to Jasper before they faded quite.

Rachel's young lady, who went often to inquire for Jasper, had not the heart to refuse the child's request, and so comforted her by reporting that she had left the daisies in Jasper's very room, where she was allowed to see the boy, and talk very quietly to him. Lest his associations with the daisies should excite him, she did not mention them as she placed them in a vase. It was no wonder that her heart was filled with pity for the sufferer.

HE SAYS.

She was an angel of consolation to that blind boy. I was the doctor who was most often with him, and I knew it. For a while, I was quite ignorant who this young lady was, and so I called her Little Her — only to myself, you understand. Where she had learned the tact to be so wise and gentle, with the often fretful boy, poor fellow! I never knew. But she grew to be such a favorite with him, that her touch, her voice, the soothing, quiet charm there was about her very presence, had more influence over him than anything or anybody else. Of course, what we doctors and nurses did for him was more or less professional; but her ways were real motherly, home-like ways. She read unexciting, short verses aloud, or talked or sang to him; and, sometimes, being nearer than she thought, I would overhear. Jasper, by no means, paid her in thanks. When she brought him hot-house flowers, he would say, in spite of his real enjoyment of the rich perfumes:

"I would rather have one of the daisies that grew at home."

And when she sang to him, one day, he only said, captiously:

"I wish I could hear Rachel sing. Not but
what you sing splendid, but I used to like
Rachel's tunes. I like to hear children sing."

"Would you really like very much to hear
a child sing?" I heard Little Her ask very
gently, in reply.

"O, yes!" he told her; "it had been so
long since he had heard a child sing."

Then she answered, "Well, dear, I will ask
the doctor, and, if he is willing, I will bring
a child I know, some day, and she shall sing
for you."

"No!" was Jasper's half-impatient reply,
"I don't want anybody strange 'round, looking
at me, when I can't look back."

"Then, when I bring this little girl," said
Little Her, cheerfully, "we'll have her sing in
the next room, or just outside the door. She
needn't see you at all."

Little Her came and asked my leave, and
I gave it. It was a pitiful thing to see that
blind boy, in his darkened room, listening

intently to the singing of a child outside his door. He did not suspect that it was his own little sister's voice.

"It was beautiful!" he said. "It was like Rachel's singing, and nothing had done him so much good, since he came from home, in the dark."

I saw the tears in the young lady's eyes, as she stood holding the boy's hand; but she would not let her voice tremble, when she answered him, brightly and tenderly as ever.

SHE SAYS.

One day Jasper was left for a few moments alone. He had been charged, on no account, to lift the bandage from his eyes, until leave was given; but an impulse of unreasonable impatience took possession of him.

"If I'm going to be blind, why shouldn't I know it now, as well as ever?" he said to himself, almost fiercely; and, not stopping to think more about it, he pushed up one corner of the linen.

His heart almost stopped beating. In that dark, still room he saw, or thought he saw, a bunch of daisies.

"O! do you suppose it is a dream?" he whispered to himself. Then, hearing a step, he pulled back the bandage, and sat down, trembling with excitement, and frightened lest he should be reproved for his wilfulness. It was only the step of a nurse, who had come to sit with him for a while.

"Are there any flowers in this room?" asked Jasper, after a few minutes.

"Yes, dear," answered the nurse, in a pitying voice, "just a bunch of daisies, dear."

Jasper said no more, except to beg for the daisies to hold.

He told nobody, for a long while, how he first found that sight was coming back, sensitively dreading the doctor's displeasure at his disobedience. But to Rachel, at last, he owned how her wish had come true; and, as the daisies had been the last flower he had seen before his blindness came upon him, so it was upon the daisies first that his restored vision fell.

For there was a glad ending to all the waiting. At last the doctors decided that Jasper was really cured. At last, with great joy, the meeting of brothers and sister took place; and plans were made for the return of the children, at Christmas, to their thankful old grandmother, who was longing to see them all.

The money saved in the tin tea-pot had held out wonderfully, all this while, so the children thought, and a grand shopping excursion, to buy Christmas presents, suggested by their friend, is still remembered by them as, probably, the happiest shopping excursion any of them ever will experience.

It was a joyful party that clambered up into the old stage, the day before Christmas, with the precious Christmas parcels and baggage. As the young lady wished to see the children safe home, her father had consented to accompany her, and spend Christmas, this year, with the good, hospitable cousins at the farm-house. As they shook hands with the admiring driver, and took their seats, it was a mutual surprise to discover Jasper's friend, the good doctor, already in his seat.

HE SAYS.

I had been invited to spend Christmas with the friend up in the country, to whom I had made a flying visit at the time when I first saw Little Her, at the covered bridge. And, stupid as it seems, until I heard Jasper, Rachel and David talking on this Christmas Eve, in the stage-coach, about the store in the covered bridge, I had not been able to trace the sensation I had felt of having met somewhere before the young lady, who had taken to coming to the hospital ward. Now it all became clear to me; and I wondered that even my busy doctor's life could have allowed me to forget so sweet and winning a woman as Little Her. How glad I was when her father courteously invited me, with my friend, to spend Christmas evening at the cousinly farm-house!

SHE SAYS.

I had never spent so happy a Christmas in all my life. It was such gladness to see the grandmother rejoicing over Jasper, and Rachel and David so brimful of delight. I had never seen Christmas presents give so much rapture as those which I had helped the children select, and a few which I added for their surprise myself.

In their hearty, open-handed way, our cousins at the farm-house would not be satisfied unless grandmother Conway and her children would join us all at the generous Christmas dinner, in neighborly cordiality. And when the doctor and his friend joined us, in the evening, the merriment, music and good cheer warmed one to the heart.

"O, how different from last year!" said Jasper, with a glad face; "last year I had to be shut up by myself while all the other children at the asylum were having a tree and good times."

"A Christmas in the dark! O, that was hard and strange," said cousin Dorothy, beaming upon Jasper in her motherly way.

HE SAYS.

But was there not something remarkable about a young and flattered lady who could thus enjoy, more than all the Christmas parties and parades of refined city life, to see a few country people happy, in a simple, old-fashioned way together?

It made so much of an impression on me that I determined to see all I could of such a character. And very fascinating I found it, but I won't tell you all about that.

But when, a year ago last Thanksgiving, Little Her — for have I not now a right to keep the old title if I please? — was married, the unreasonable little bride could not be content to return from her wedding journey till she had once more taken that same old ride in the jolting stage-coach, and spent a day at the ample cousinly farm-house. And when the familiar, covered bridge was reached, what a surprise was there! For the cousins had passed the word, and Rachel, Jasper and David could not do enough to show how glad they were for the dear young lady, who had taken such pains for them. From end to end that bridge was lined gaily with great boughs of cedar, hemlock, laurel and pine ; garlands festooned it, twined with great care, and scarlet berries intermingled with the green.

At the windows of the little red Conway house, eager faces were looking out, handkerchiefs were waved from the door, kisses were tossed from Rachel's finger-tips. The blushing bride was so overpowered that she was truly glad to have the stage sweep by with the grand flourish and feint of hurry which the stage-driver got up for the occasion.

Not that she was displeased with the children's demonstrations in her honor, as they must have been well assured when, the following Christmas, they received the big box which she insisted on sending them.)(

SHE SAYS.

Well, and what more natural than to try to make the succeeding Christmases of Jasper, and the rest, all the brighter for that one dreary Christmas in the dark?

There! it is a woman's right always to have the last word.

"O! read mine next! do read mine next!" besought Mollie Periwinkle, putting in her claim in a great hurry, before this plum had been thoroughly discussed; "please, mamma, read it for me. I know it's cousin Red's handwriting, but I haven't learned pen-letters yet. Mamma may read it, mayn't she, cousin Red?"

Cousin Red nodded smiling; and Mollie's mother, with Mollie nestling close up to her, untied the scarlet ribbons about the packet which Mollie had snatched from the Pie.

"It looks like a delicious plum," said Mollie, gleefully, pretending to sniff at it, as the reading began.

CHAPTER IX.

PLUM THE FOURTH.

"IT'S one of the prettiest sights I ever 'ave 'ad the pleasure of seein'," Toby the footman gave as his august opinion, from his station in front of the great kitchen range.

He had just come down from above stairs gorgeous in his scarlet plush and buff waistcoat, his well-fitting pumps and white neckcloth, come down ostensibly to describe the guests, but more particularly for a "pull" at one of the short, plethoric jugs of ale that garnished the kitchen dresser.

189

The cook and the housekeeper's maid looked up to say:

"Well now, really! this is werry fine of you, Toby;" which commendation led him to stand still a second or so after having emptied the little tankard, and wipe the white foam from his mouth, and wink cunningly at the butler who, across the dresser, was fumbling the wine-cellar keys.

"Ay, the picture gallery with hits green baize curting, hits stage and hall. Hits fine, though! Miss Ethelred's bright curls a-bobbin' through the 'alls, hand 'er father hand 'er old aunt so proud of 'er. Then them tablets, hor wotever hit is they're to do, will be grand enough. Hi just got the lad as the confectioner sent in to wait hat table, to mind the 'all door, thinking 'ow as hi would slip down and tell you to creep hup onto the staircase by and by, hand 'ave a peep hat the fun, honly —"

Here the great bell rang so loudly that

Toby cut short his intended speech, and hastened, with great dignity, out of the kitchen;
for, despite his love for gossiping with his
fellow-servants, he appreciated too keenly the
importance of this, the first great family
party which his young mistress had ever
given, to keep any guest waiting long upon
the frosty steps of the great house in the
Square.

"As to that 'ere confectioner's boy, he might
be a-stuffin' 'isself with cakes and sweetmeats
behind the dining-room door, for all 'e knew.
Confectioners' boys they was so werry hodd,
they was."

Up-stairs how the lights gleamed on brave
old English holly, and Christmas wreaths and
mottoes! What a goodly company of papas,
mammas, uncles, aunts; aye, and happy looking grandpas and grandmas, with little flossy
heads and blue English eyes hiding behind
their arm-chairs, were gathered together. Laces
and stiff brocades, and glowing bits of gems,

like little chips of a royal rainbow, sifted through the room.

The ruddy fire-light beamed a welcome to all, and now fragrant coffee began to be handed about in quaint, antique china cups.

Approving glances followed the young hostess, Ethelred, as, with matronly care for their comfort, she flitted about among her guests.

Very graceful she was, in her rich yet simple dress, and the innocent, girlish face had the wistful look of one shielded thus far from knowledge of the world, while yet a spirit that could prove brave and firm when tested, gazed from the soft eyes. Even the servants of the house looked after her with a certain loving pride in their proprietor-like glances.

At last the guests were summoned from the drawing-rooms to the picture-gallery at the top of the house, where that mystic baize curtain screened the magic wonders from the children's eyes, and the tableaux began.

The long and charming evening wore away;

Ethelred as Red Ridinghood.
194

the little heads without the curtain leaned on friendly shoulders, and charades, and music, and lights began to lose themselves and grow very far away, when a concluding drama was announced, "for the children;" a drama that was to be all about the old but ever witching Red Ridinghood.

Behind the scenes a gay group laughed and chattered in half merry, half repressed frolic, while they acted as tire-women to Red Ridinghood herself, and then the curtain rose.

Ethelred stood there, under the softened lights, in her short brown stuff dress, with her tiny feet in scarlet shoes, and her almost too childish little figure draped in the long folds of an ancient red cloak, her bright, nebulous hair falling loosely from out the hood.

"O! *isn't* she tunnin'?" lisped one of the sleepy little children, roused quite awake at the sight.

And a young artist, who was leaning against the door-way, studying the picture, smiled and thought to himself, " I wonder if there is in all England to-night, a prettier sight than little Ethelred in her great grandmother's scarlet cloak."

He remembered the day when they had been exploring the great cedar-chest for its long-hoarded velvet gowns, stiff brocades, faded satins and last century's bonnets, while she planned for this evening's entertainment.

Ethelred had taken this very scarlet cloak from the chest, shaking it out merrily, with a laugh at its old-fashioned splendor.

A sunbeam from the narrow window fell across the dim, still old garret, transfiguring with its dusty goldenness that small figure in its scarlet drapery and bright flossy hair, and bringing out that wistful, innocent look in Ethelred's eyes, which was just what the child Red Ridinghood might have had.

" It is the very thing!" cried young Philip, " Ethelred's knight and neighbor," as he had always called himself since they were children

together. "I will write a little play for you,
Ethelred; you shall be Red Ridinghood, and
then I will paint you in that character. I
wonder I have not thought of it before, for
I've never been suited with any of the names
I've painted you under."

It had been delightful — the writing of the
fanciful little drama, and then the rehearsing
of it; and the heroine took her part so well
that the young people all followed Philip's
lead, and, leaving off the stately Ethel from
her name, called her, most of the time, nothing but "Red," unless they called her Red
Ridinghood in full.

To-night, as Philip stood watching her, she
crossed to him, her wicker basket, with its
little butter-pat, on her arm, and said playfully :

"If they clamor for the author of all this
pretty drama I shall come to lead you out,
Sir Philip. We must have our little Red
Ridinghood properly appreciated, you know."

With a sudden impulsive tenderness he bent down to her, saying:

"Red Ridinghood, my own darling little Red Ridinghood, you know very well that I should go wherever you wanted to lead me."

He took her hand eagerly, and went on, "O Red Ridinghood, let me —"

"Ethelred!"

Her father's voice, peculiarly emphatic, and with a nameless grave displeasure in it, interrupted the hurrying words on his lips. Starting, she left him to answer her father's call, a blush of surprise — or was it anger? — upon her fair face. She left him standing by the staircase door.

He cared little for the success of his cunningly-plotted play. He knew they laughed and applauded; that cries of ecstasy came shrilly from childish lips, that all went on victoriously. But he seemed only to see the scarlet-cloaked girl, and the wistful look that deepened and grew to sadness in her eyes.

He did not see her again. Very unexpectedly Ethelred went to spend the remaining holidays among distant relatives, and Philip was not a little piqued that she did not send for him to say good-by. He did not know that the prudent, worldly-wise father, startled by the lover-like looks last night between the two, had suddenly awakened to realize that they were no longer the children together he had been fancying them.

"This mischief must go no farther," he had said promptly to himself, " for what is this boy? Only the orphan nephew of my neighbor, crotchety Squire Rodney, who may yet change his mind and disinherit him. Only a dreamy, artist sort of fellow, too. Better things are in store for my daughter and heiress than that. His uncle told me that he means to send Philip to Germany to study. I will advice his going — in a friendly way — at once; and, meanwhile, Ethelred shall accept the invitation she received yesterday."

The prudent father had his way. Before Ethelred's return Philip had gone abroad, and when he came back to old England — but we're getting ahead of our story, and that is as bad as eating all the plums out of one Christmas Pie at once!

He went abroad, a little angry with Red Ridinghood, as I said, and yet somehow he forgot the anger, because he could not forget her. Whenever he saw the sunlight glinting on a scarlet cloak, he turned to look again at it; but the foreign face that looked from under the hood, was never so beautiful or so true as the little Red Ridinghood he left in England.

Aye, and sometime he would yet paint her, as he remembered her, he always told himself. When he became a rich and famous artist he would paint her just as she stood in that old, gray garret, with its one dusty sunbeam for a background.

But I fancy that when Ethelred leaned her

head down a little wearily that Christmas Eve night, as she knelt at her prayers, she thought far less of the brilliant, successful evening than she did of the old scarlet cloak, lying on a chair beside her. Hiding her face in its folds, she dreamed over it, perhaps, as her great grandmother might have done before her, and resolved, in her foolish little heart, never to part with it, for the sake of the sweet, untold story that it meant to her.

Without, the pallid Christmas light struggled faintly through, the old bells of St. Christopher's chimed over the white, white earth, the coming of the glad and glorious King of Peace. The last clash of sound, like a spray of dewdrops falling, echoed and re-echoed faintly.

Toby heard it. He had just put out the last taper, and locked the hall door after the last guest; only, this time, it was that same confectioner's boy whom he had found fast asleep in a dining-chair behind the door, and had shaken broad awake with a fierce, exultant pleasure, and a—

"See 'ere, you boy! W'en hi ketches you hat them cream tarts again, mind, hi'll get you a safer place than this, 'ere in a gentleman's dining-room, to digest 'em in!"

And had so frightened the poor lad that it was from watching him as he ran distractedly down the chill, empty street, and round the old church corner, that Toby now drew in his head with a quiet chuckle.

What did he care for the bells in the white dawn? They rang a carol of hope and a song of peace for Ethelred, as she listened, and forgot the fluttering of her one poor heart in the reverent memory of a rejoicing that embraced earth and heaven in its gladness; but to Toby, they meant only—four o'clock on a cold Christmas morning. So different are these hearts of ours!

While Ethelred went to sleep with a prayer on her lips, Toby, as he locked and bolted the wide hall door, kept a close eye on the silver basket, and shook his head, muttering:

"Confectioners' boys they was so werry uncommon hodd, they was."

And so ended another Christmas Eve.

Now I will tell you that when Red Ridinghood's lover, Philip, came hopefully back from his study abroad, no Red Ridinghood was there to welcome him home. I do not like to tell you what sore troubles had fallen on that bright head of hers.

Her father, though he had been a man whom everybody trusted, had been drawn into speculations, had failed in them, had tried to retrieve his footing by rash and dishonest means, and then, fearing to face certain disgrace, had fled in selfish cowardice across the ocean, for a while no one knew where. Poor Red Ridinghood took refuge where she could; but all was very different now, and many who had seemed her friends avoided her now, as if to punish her for the sin of her

father. After some months the poor, weak
father wrote a pitiful letter, begging her to
come to him in America.

The relatives who had been kind to her,
and given her a home, forbade her to go; and
bitterly declared that if she did go of her
own choice to join the man who had dishon-
ored the family name by such a shameful
deed, they would disown her as utterly as
they did him.

But faithful Ethelred was firm in that which
she believed to be her filial duty. Her
father had said that he was sick and wretched,
and needed her. He had plead with her to
come, in the name of her dead mother. So
she went, though sorely pained that the sacri-
fice, which was no light one, should anger and
estrange her few remaining friends.

Thus set out our Little Red Ridinghood on
her way through the woods. And she found
it a hard way. And she even met the wolf;
for, bravely as she worked to support herself

and her father, when he became a helpless invalid, full of vain remorse and self-reproach, sometimes poverty came close to the brave maiden, and showed his teeth threateningly. Little Red Ridinghood learned to bear being lonesome, and tired, and even hungry, and yet to seem cheerful and to keep hopeful, and never in her heart to be despairing, however downcast she might get, but trust that some day she would get out of the woods, and that all the way through the Lord would surely take care of her.

One day she came upon a copy of the little old play of Red Ridinghood, which she had kept carefully, and brought with her over the seas. It had her name written on the fly-leaf, as Philip used to write it in sport, "Ethel Red."

"Am I the same one who played Red Ridinghood that night?" she thought to herself. "I feel quite like another person."

But she smiled and blushed over the crumpled leaves, much like the same Ethel Red.

Meanwhile Philip could find no trace of her, since her proud relatives would receive no letters from father or daughter, and did not know their whereabouts.

Another Christmas Eve had come round, and this time it found Philip at his sister's home in America. While he had been adopted by his uncle in England, this sister, older than he, had married early and removed to America, so that the two were almost strangers to each other until their present meeting.

Philip was sitting alone that afternoon with a new book open before him. Its type was clear and faultless, the most acute critics had approved it as learned and eloquent. Yet the reader had scarcely turned a half-dozen pages. He had opened to the fly-leaf, and was sketching rapidly, half-unconsciously, the outlines of a weird picture. A forest, a haunted forest, with grotesque forms hiding behind its trees, strange faces peeping down from the branches overhead, and back where the outline of a narrow, winding path began the figure of one who stood looking sadly down it as if in baffled search.

"Uncle Philip!"

Princess really felt a burden of responsibility resting upon her this afternoon. To be sure, their first Christmas in the new house out in the country was very delightful, and it was pleasant to have company to keep it with them. But it was so hard to keep the little children away from the locked parlor door, while all the grown folks were busy inside at the grand mystery which was to be revealed on the morrow! Mamma had particularly charged her with the care of the smaller guests, and Princess, having tried to be very polite and entertaining, felt her resources quite exhausted when it began to snow, and the fun out-of-doors was suspended.

Princess turned it all over in her anxious mind, and concluded on this step at last; for, new as this uncle was to the children, they had already found out that he could tell delicious stories. Having made up her mind, Princess never faltered nor stammered.

"Uncle Philip, I wish you would be so kind as to tell the children a story. I cannot think of anything else to amuse them, and, of course, it is my duty to look out for them while mamma is so busy. They *will* keep peeping in at the parlor key-hole."

At his petitioner's anxious, matronly air, and the perplexed wrinkle in her clear forehead, uncle Philip threw away book and pencil, and said, briskly:

"My dear Princess, command your subjects here immediately. I **am** in just the mood for story-telling."

All the young people gathered around him gaily, the smallest child, curly-headed Ernest, perching on the story-teller's knee, and Princess sitting at his feet.

He looked at her expectant, upraised face,

as the group, with a hum of exclamation and
gratulation, noisily drew up chairs, or nes-
tled down on cushions; while the ˙fire-light
went on flickering in the grate, and painting
against the white snow-light of that Christmas
Eve, warm, rich tints. He saw only serious,
fearless blue eyes, clear as light; a low, wo-
manly brow; a mouth gathered firmly at the
corners, whereby one would have read her
fit to trust with a secret, child as she was;
and pale cheeks, softly rounded, not apt to
crimson except sometimes with a faint flush
like that you see in pearl. Only this, yet, as
if he saw more, uncle Philip gazed dreamily
down into the child's eyes.

"All ready, now, Uncle Philip!"

Still looking into Princess' eyes, he began
without preface:

"Little Red Ridinghood set out on her
walk through the woods."

"O! don't tell us that old, old Red Ridinghood!" chorused the tall Miss Josephine,

just beginning to see over her mamma's head, and the manly Arthur, who was half way through the Latin Reader.

"O! don't tell us Red Ridinghood!" begged timid Elizabeth. "Nurse told it to us only last night, all about the basket of butter, and how she said, 'What a great mouth you've got!' and he snapped her right up, — and I dreamed about it all night myself, and Ernest screamed out in his sleep that he'd swallowed her down as far as the basket, but the butter stuck in his throat!"

"O! do tell us Red Ridinghood," with a little shiver, and eyes shining brighter, from Ernest, at the head of the very little ones of the party.

In no wise disconcerted, uncle Philip merely smiled mysteriously, and repeated :

"Little Red Ridinghood set out on her walk through the woods. There was one who went with her to the edge of the woods, but there his path branched off from hers. Just as she stepped under the pines, where there was a little path over the snow, the sun broke through the massive clouds that were piled up in the sky, and made little Red Riding-hood look so lovely and so bright, as she stood there turning to wave good-by, that he who had come thus far with her said to him-self, 'Beautiful Little Red Ridinghood! I won-der if there is a fairy of fire-light, for you look just like such a being. God bless you, God take care of you, Little Red Riding-hood!'

"Red Ridinghood did not know she looked so fair. As she went on into the shady path, leaving the sunbeam behind, she sang softly to herself a song that she had heard her mother sing.

> " 'Wherever His child-folks may go,
> The Lord doth lead them, this I know;
> And we are vain to think that we
> Can lead them safer than can He.

> " 'Wherever His child-folks may go,
> The Lord doth love them, this I know;

And we are vain to think that we
Can love them better than can He.'

"Red Ridinghood caught sight of a trailing green vine shining up through the fleece of the snow. She pulled at a bit of it, but no long spray would follow; the frosty stem broke in her hand. However, she would not stop to try again, for her mother bade her not to delay for anything in the woods. So she went swiftly on with the one fragment in her hand, though she would have liked a handful to fill the vase that stood empty, she knew, on her grandmother's table. God was pleased with her for obeying without questioning and He sent her a sweet thought to keep her company.

"'God will have white carpets like the snow on our floors in Heaven perhaps,' she thought, as she looked down at the foot-prints she had made in the snow; 'and *then* my feet will be too clean to soil them.'

"The foot-prints followed her as she walked

steadily on, the shadows followed her too, creeping along behind her, gently and noise-lessly at first, then racing with her and getting beyond her. She held her basket tight.

" Some snow-birds wished each other a merry Christmas under the pine rafters, with their drooping green tassels over her head, and then came down and hopped along before her, hopeful and gay.

" Again Red Ridinghood hummed to herself;

> " ' God's things should always dare to be
> Glad and free, glad and free;
> He cares for all, and cares if He
> A light, brave heart doth find in me.

> " ' Close to us, He doth look to see
> If so we can rest happily;
> For if with Him we be not glad,
> What more in Heaven can be had ? '

" A rabbit leaped nimbly over the path; a squirrel ran into his nest in a hollow tree, and the shadows crowded around Red Ridinghood, for the woods grew darker and denser.

"And then it was that something blacker than the gloom, more stealthy than the shadows, crept through the dimness of the woods' arches and came close to Little Red Ridinghood. She shivered a little, but she looked bravely into the wolf's eyes when he met her, (would you have done so, Princess?) and somehow he did not have voice at first to say anything but 'Good evening.'

"'Good evening,' answered Red Ridinghood, in her clear, Sunday-bell voice.

"'A lonesome wood,' said the wolf, politely.

"'I am not lonesome,' replied Red Ridinghood quietly; 'in the woods all live in love, one with another'—here the wolf stared.

"'What great eyes you've got!' cried Red Ridinghood, breaking off abruptly.

"'To see the better with,' said the wolf, as if with an effort; 'go on.'

"'And besides,' continued Red Ridinghood, 'it is Christmas Eve.'

"'What's the difference of that?' asked the wolf, with dilating nostrils.

"'What a great nose you've got!' exclaimed Red Ridinghood, innocently wondering.

"'To smell the better with; go on, I say,' repeated the wolf, impatiently.

"'Why! on Christmas night, years ago, while the shepherds took care of their white sheep, in the starlight, suddenly there appeared,' and Red Ridinghood, folding her hands, repeated the words of the chant, which all the school-children had been learning, to sing to-morrow in the church: 'A multitude of the heavenly host, praising God, and saying, "Glory to God in the highest, and on earth peace, good-will towards men." And the Babe Jesus was born across the sea, in Bethlehem of Judea, to be our Redeemer. So now we keep his birthday, sir, with feasting, and joy, and singing; and surely, then, one need not fear that, in the green woods, aught can hurt or kill.'

"'I am hungry,' said the wolf, his jaws

working nervously; 'if you've such great good-will to the universe, give me — what have you there, fit for your Christmas feasting? Give it me.'

"'O! but I cannot,' said faithful Little Red Ridinghood; 'it is a little Christmas gift for my dear grandmamma, and mother bade me guard it well — O! what a great mouth you've got!' she screamed in affright, as the wolf grinned fiendishly.

"'To eat you the better with!' was the wolf's fierce, angry answer, and he sprang towards poor Little Red Ridinghood.

"O! how she ran now, yet remembered to grasp tightly the basket of butter. O! how fast the wolf ran behind her, how fearfully fast.

" How close he was getting! His panting breath felt hot, he was so near.

"She felt his grip; he tore the long, scarlet cloak from her shoulder. Was it all over with poor Little Red Ridinghood?

"No; the cloak entangled his reckless feet; he stumbled, and, as he fell, his head hit violently against a jagged, projecting stump, that, I think, must have been glad then to be only an old broken stump of God's, and there he lay, stunned and blinded, with the scarlet cloak all crumpled up about him.

"But Little Red Ridinghood fled on and on, not hearing him groan, not looking behind her, and reached all safe, with the basket of butter, the little low house on the edge of the pine woods, where her grandmother lived.

"A last sunbeam lit up her tumbled golden hair as she stood on tip-toe to lift the latch of the door, and she heard her grandmother's trembling voice crooning within:

> " ' " One thing I know; God keeps his own;
> Where'er they live, they're not alone;
> Where'er they walk, though fears press **near**,
> He is between them and all fear.

> " ' " One thing I know; God keeps his own,
> And he can do it all alone;
> We, being absent, need not fear,
> But he does as well for our dear." ' "

The door opened, and the hostess herself came in, hurriedly.

"Well done, Uncle Philip!" said she as she surveyed the flower-bed of listening children; "but I have not time to applaud, for our evergreens have given out at this late hour, and we really must have a wreath or two more. Could you go to the woods with Michael, Philip, for one more load?"

"Certainly," said her brother, rising promptly, and, putting on his overcoat, he watched the children scatter, like beads rolling off a broken string, let us hope *not* under the parlor keyhole.

"Please, please let me go, too, mamma!" begged Ernest.

"O, no, my child! why, it's snowing!" answered the prudent mother.

"It was a mere snow-shower," interposed uncle Philip, pitying the disappointed tears that filled Ernests' beseeching eyes. "See! it is really clearing up. Wrap the boy up, and trust him to me."

So away they went, down the drive-way, through the wide, sleepy village street, past the simple country church, standing significant in silence, with uplifted spire, and, finally, up the cart-path that led away from the cross-road. As Dolly stepped slower, coming in among the dark pines, Ernest ceased his glee-ful chatter, and drew closer to his companion, thinking of Red Ridinghood's adventures, as he had just heard them. And his uncle was silent, too. Was he pondering subjects far more weighty and solemn than Ernest had in mind? Was he recalling the lore of Germany, remembering reverent hours in solemn cathe-drals, planning for the future? Did he think of that first Christmas, centuries ago, and all it imported?

Afterwards he owned that the thoughts which absorbed him were none of these. He was only dwelling on a vision of a girl who stood in a dim, dusty garret, wrapped in the fire-glow of her great-grandmother's scarlet

cloak, with a single ray of sunshine lighting
up her changeful hair, and vivifying the
deep-tinted folds, that fell about her so care-
lessly.

"O, my Little Red Ridinghood!" he was
saying to himself, "am I never to know how
you came through the woods? And what may
have befallen you!"

"These be the hemlocks, sir;" broke in
Michael's gruff voice. "Whoa, Dolly!"

Philip shook off the dreamy mood, really
half ashamed of it, and helped to load the
wagon with fragrant boughs so energetically
that Michael's respect for him was very much
raised. How still it was in the woods! With
the light caressing of the brief afternoon's
snow laid evenly upon them, the evergreens
stood, in a hush that was like a breathless,
expectant waiting for something to come.

A shrill cry startled the busy workers.

"O Uncle Philip! Uncle Philip! it is Red
Ridinghood and she will meet the wolf. Do
go with her! Do take care of her!"

They turned quickly, first to Ernest, as he stood with lips apart, and eager eyes, upon the hillock of green they had piled up in the wagon, then following his pointing finger to an opening through the trees.

There, under the canopy of pines that bent courtly about her, stood outlined against the pure snow a little figure in an ancient scarlet cloak, with a basket on her arm.

One sunset sunbeam from the western sky, where at evening time it was light, flickered on the slender form in its faded red. She turned at the sound of voices, and looked at them with the very wistful, half-startled eyes of Red Ridinghood herself.

"An' shure, mem," said Michael, in the parlor, glad of an excuse to linger over the last handful of hemlock, and admire the stately tree and the transfigured walls; "it's more than I know mesilf, mem, where he wint, at ahl. Faith, but I thought mesilf at first, mem, 'twas something uncanny had bewitched him, a-rushin' off white-like, widout a word, an' me not darin' to wait, knowin' ye was in a hurry, mem. Och! it's sure I am that I nivir see the likes of her, mem, nor the red cloak of her, since we came here."

"Very strange!" ejaculated his mistress, as she shut the door after Michael, and went herself to untie Ernest's tippet in the hall.

"But I know all about it, mamma," whispered Ernest, confidentially; "it's Red Ridinghood, that's all, and uncle Philip has only gone to get her away from the wolf!"

Ah! little had our Red Ridinghood guessed what would happen when she had put on the red cloak, thinking that surely she would meet nobody if she took the path through the woods in the twilight, while certainly, the sick woman at the edge of the woods, for whom she had been able to make up a little basket of Christmas cheer, "just because she was English," Ethelred explained, would not mind her unaccustomed garb.

True, she did like the feeling of the cloak once more about her, and could not help a smile and a tear at the memory of that bright Christmas Eve in Mother England; but there was still the practical reason for her wearing it, that she had really, poor little thing, nothing else as warm.

And, lo! as if there had been some enchantment about it, the very knight she was dreaming about, half unconsciously, looking familiar yet unfamiliar, and speaking in the same remembered voice, strode down the woods to meet her, and, checking his impetuosity, said softly and chivalrously, as any knight should:

" Red Ridinghood, dear Little Red Ridinghood, may I go with you through the woods?"

It was no great wonder that, when Red Ridinghood's knight found out how hard a time she had had, he should declare that his life's great Christmas gift should never have an hour's more lonely walk through haunted forests, while he could take care of her.

"My Ethel Red," he said, with his old impulsiveness, "you shall marry me to-morrow!"

The little woman in the red cloak blushed, and shrank, and said: "O no! why, I have not even a gown good enough to be married in, Philip!" and stopped overwhelmed in confusion, blushing red indeed.

"I don't want you to marry me in anything better than the red cloak," persisted the unreasonable lover, firmly. "It is far better than any wedding silk that ever bride was decked in, and red cloak and all I will, I will have you, Ethel, Ethel Red, for my Christmas gift!"

Thus all Little Red Ridinghood's loneliness came to an end.

"There, now! wasn't my plum nice?" asked Mollie, clapping her hands, as her mother stopped reading. "I knew it would be nice, when I saw cousin Red's handwriting."

"But what does it mean?" said Ronald, puzzled; "do you mean that you were Red Ridinghood yourself, cousin Red? Is that the reason we call you cousin Red?"

"Not quite that," she answered, "but my own mother was the Red Ridinghood of the story, and I have heard the tale told over so many times, that it seems as though I had seen it all happen, myself. And when they named me after my mother, my father insisted on writing it in two words; so that abroad I was called Ethel, and at home I was called Red. Whose plum next?"

"Will you have mine?" asked uncle Brederode, holding up the written sheets in his hand. But, as the little boy opposite him cried out: "Mine! mine!" at the same moment, he said, laughing, "Well, I'm bigger than you, my boy; you shall have your turn first!"

So, at the child's appealing look, Mr. Sylverner read.

CHAPTER X.

PLUM THE FIFTH.

THE night was closing in fast, and the good horse was near wearied out, but now the rough Australian inn towards which he had been all day hard pushed, had come in sight.

"Ho! old fellow; wake up! we're almost there!" and, at the rider's good-natured slap on his flank, the animal, seeming quite to understand, pricked up his sharp ears gallantly, and spurred on.

From weariness, however, he was again

226

subsiding into his dogged trot, when the distant sound of other hoofs approaching reached his quick senses before it did his master's, and he roused again to a clumsy gallop.

The tramping of horse's feet came on swiftly, and presently three or four riders, dimly discernible through the dusk, rounded an abrupt bend of the road.

"Good evening, stranger," said the gruff voice of the foremost horseman.

"Good evening, gentlemen!" returned our traveller, courteously.

"You're for the inn yonder?"

"I am — as I conclude you are," was the reply; "we shall arrive together."

"And lucky we're so near, too," another voice broke in; "there's a storm brewing, or all the signs are wrong. From far, stranger?"

"Well, a fair stretch for one day," the traveller answered, curtly.

He knew that there was need to be on his guard, and had no mind to enlighten these unauthorized catechists on his own affairs. But of this very reticence his companions made a note, and, under cover of the deepening shadows, sinister looks passed among them, as they dismounted at the low-roofed inn.

Later, as the guests sat around the glowing logs in the fire-place, all that redeemed the dingy, dirty room, where the supper of rude abundance was served, the traveller noted in his turn an attempt at coarse and boisterous friendliness on the part of the strangers. This he was careful not to repulse, whether it might mean good or ill; but he was careful, also, not to be betrayed into confidence or familiarity.

As the evening wore on, and the storm which had been brewing without, burst, it became plain that sleep and silence were not to settle down early within.

The landlord and a couple of his boon companions were added to the number of the revellers, and the place rang with their hoarse laughter, broad jesting and coarse revelry, liquor passing more and more freely around. The traveller had declined a share in all this, evidently not much to the good will of those about him; and finding writing, sleeping, well-nigh thinking impossible, he threw himself down on a hard bench, and closed his eyes, to get what rest he might till the tumult should subside.

He was very tired. I think, in spite of the noise, he fell into a succession of slight dozes; for once, when he opened his eyes, it was from a vision very different from this barbarous hut, with its shaggy beams, its smoky air, its unkempt barrenness, and the great boar's head over the door.

A child's voice had been speaking to him; he had been looking into a child's innocent face, soft, pure and high-bred, come of races born to luxury.

He opened his eyes, as I said, and there seemed to be sitting near him a small shape, that might be a child.

Not the child he had been dreaming about, his pet during a stay in England, not the little Saxon Countess Genevieve, safe in her stately, ancestral home — O, no!

And, if it were a child in size, this figure sat more like an old man, stooping, listless, heavy. It was strangely, uncouthly dressed, and had wiry, bristling black hair. Was it a child? wondered the traveller, half-awake.

A louder shout, and this time a torrent of angry oaths came from the bar-room.

The shape, or shadow, which the traveller had been looking at, coughed a hollow, agonizing cough; and a half-groan, that, alas! was an oath, too, followed it.

The traveller rose, and, going up to the shadow, saw that it did, indeed, take the form of a child, crouching on an untanned skin, which. he had dragged there before the smouldering fire.

But, alas, for such a child!

His face had the sharpened outline, the starveling expression of the wolf, and yet, not the wolf's acute intelligence, its clean-cut shape.

Weazen, and worn and weirdly aged it looked; utterly "Ignorant of all grace, refinement, purity, but too wise in all that knowledge which can sear and shrivel the mind.

This face it was which turned towards the traveller a look so suspicious and scowling that it was almost malignant, when he asked, kindly:

"Is it not very late, my boy? Why are you up?"

"Business of yours, is it?" rejoined the boy, sharply, almost like a snarling dog.

The traveller tried another subject.

"You have a bad cough. Do you take no medicine for it?"

"What is it to you?" retorted the snarl again, so angrily, that the traveller, repulsed, kept silence. But the cough would not so easily and summarily be silenced. It returned again and again, and even the young stoic could not disguise, from the on-looker, that, with the cough, came sharp darts of pain, that stabbed chest and side. As long as he could, the sufferer morosely refused the sympathy and aid which humanity impelled his companion to offer. Still, pain can tame a very wolf itself; and such pain this wolfish boy had never known before, as the pleurisy which evidently had griped him now.

"Have you no mother? Cannot I call her?" asked the stranger.

"Never had one," answered the sick boy, between his rasping breaths.

"Then your father — is he here? Let me bring him."

"You *are* green!" was the derisive reply, given with an oath.

But, without waiting for it, the other had already sought the revellers, only to find it too true, that help from these drunken beasts, now half-stupified, was, indeed, vain to expect. Upon this he took matters into his own hands. With a resolution, from which there was no appeal, he laid his strange patient on a couch, hastily contrived, and forced him to swallow remedies, which, in his wandering life, he carried about with him. Beginning to feel a certain elation, in conquering the effort at sullen resistance with which the patient met every measure, he tried every means to relieve the suffering which his experience could suggest. At last, worn out by pain, and thoroughly subdued by the stronger will, the half-savage boy yielded to everything proposed by his physician, with a meek docility, so new, so almost child-like in contrast, that his conqueror felt it strangely pathetic. When he slept, brokenly, relieved by warmth and care, the man watching by him, looked pitifully at the white face of this neglected piece of childhood, and, brushing back the tangled

locks, smoothed, as gently as if it had been
Genevieve's own, the forehead which seemed
not destitute of promise, beneath the bushy
disguise of hair.

The house had, at last, grown still; but
the sick boy tossed restlessly on his couch,
and, waking from disturbed snatches of sleep,
put out his hand gropingly, as if in appeal,
like any poor, sick child.

"Shall I tell you stories, my lad, to make
the time shorter, since you cannot sleep?"
asked the involuntary physician, compassionately, as he took the hard, grimy hand in a
firm, friendly grasp.

For, in wakeful nights, far away in the old
homestead, well he remembered the charm of
his mother's stories. And, when he tried it
on this ignorant, uncared-for boy, he found
here, too, the charm work.

He lay more quietly, the grimy hand even,
if, at times withdrawn, straying back finally to
the hand of his friend, and a human look of

interest stealing, more and more, into the eyes that had been so dull and animal.

The story-teller himself grew interested in his experiment. He began with a bear story, and then he narrated bits from the Arabian Nights, and then slipped over into Robinson Crusoe. Bits of spirited poetry suggested themselves, and fragments of nursery fable. But, by and by, from the force of association, some old stories out of the Bible came back to his memory, just as his mother used to tell them; and he grew more absorbed in telling, his hearer more absorbed in listening.

"I never heard it before," said the boy once, in simple wonder.

And again:

"Are there such things, really? We never knew it."

So it went on until a quieter sleep overpowered the boy; the story-teller's voice, too, died away. With his head on his hands, he slept till day.

Uncomfortable as the place was, our traveller had a reason for remaining a few days in it.

He was collecting a volume of researches concerning the country, and he had some important observations to gather and to record, from this point, near a mining region, which interested him.

This was not his first experience at roughing it; and, becoming engrossed in his work, he paid little heed to his surroundings, the character of the food, cooked by a cross old crone, or the villainous-looking men who hung about the inn.

There was, ever after the first night, a peculiarity in the tenacity with which the boy, whom all the men called Jim, silently attached himself to his physician.

So like the fidelity of a tamed animal was that with which he followed and obeyed his friend if he moved, or sat mutely watching him while he studied or wrote, that his first idea concerning him continued to haunt that gentleman's mind, and he fell into the habit of calling him, "My Wolf." The boy's father, the landlord of the inn, paid little attention to him, being evidently without love for him, and yet aware, as he frankly informed the traveller, that "The boy had a devil in him, and it was too much trouble to fight it."

There came another dark and lowering night. The inn was unusually quiet early that evening, and the traveller, as he toiled over his accumulating sheets of MSS., supposed it must be owing to this fact that he found himself growing so heavily and unconquerably drowsy.

Unable to resist he threw himself, as he was, on his pallet, intending, after he had rested awhile, to rise and finish enough of his task to allow him to proceed on his way with the morrow.

Profoundly, unnaturally he slept, till he seemed to be dreaming that the sharp teeth of a wolf were tearing at him, pulling fiercely at his clothes. A stupor, which he could not throw off, still oppressed him.

With the struggles of the wolf, he was sure he heard Jim's voice: "Come! come! only come!"

Powerless to understand this nightmare phantasy, yet too passive to resist, he allowed himself to be dragged along.

Dully he perceived that the boy — or was it the wolf? — had, clutched in one hand, the MSS. on which he had seen bestowed so many hours of labor. Dully he heard the frantic tone in which he was besought still to "Come! come! only come!"

Yielding, as yet stupidly, he found himself borne on, with the excited boy panting at his side, he knew not whither.

It was in a secluded forest spot that they paused; and, crying piteously, "O, wake up! wake up! you must wake up!" the boy dashed cold water from the brook in his companion's face, and chafed his hands, until he,

who had been like one walking in his sleep,
began to return to his senses.

"What does this mean, Wolf?" he said,
with that accent of mastership which he had
assumed with the boy.

"O! they gave you something to make you
sleep! they meant to rob you — or worse,"
cried Wolf, breathless. "And I heard them
plan. You must ride away — away! See! I led
your horse here first. Go! quick! quick!
They may find us out!"

"I am not afraid; tell me all about it,"
said the man coolly.

"No, no! don't ask me! don't stay! They
believe you have money about you, and they
say they hate your proud ways. O! do go!"

"And leave you, Wolf?" asked his friend.

"Yes, only go!" persisted Wolf, fixed in
his one idea; "for, if I am not asleep in my
bunk before the time they've set to come,
they will blame it on me, and I shall be
killed instead of you!"

Suspicious signs, that Wolf's story might be too true, came back now to the intended victim's mind; looks unnoticed yesterday, a whisper half-heard, the strange drowsiness that had possessed him.

For Wolf's sake, and his own, he acted quickly.

"Will you go with me, Wolf?" he asked abruptly.

"No, no," said the boy, sadly, "I must not."

"Then, my brave Wolf, good bye."

He pressed a ring he wore into the lad's hand, and hurriedly wrote his home address, on a leaf torn from his pocket-book.

"Keep both these, Wolf," he said, putting his hand on Wolf's shoulder, and looking into his eyes with his own somewhat dim; "and, though you cannot write, poor boy! if I can ever do anything for you, send a letter to this name and place. Perhaps you have saved my life. The God I have told you about bless

you for it! And, Wolf, promise me that if
ever you get into trouble and need help you
will try to find me. Do you promise?"

"Yes," said the boy, trembling, "only go!
go!"

Down the forest path trampled the feet of
the horse; up the forest path hurried the
feet of the boy, swiftly, stealthily, back to the
den he called home.

Once the horse's rider looked back. The
boy, fumbling at his neck, to hide away the
ring, was also looking back. More than ever
the retreating traveller was struck with the
resemblance the face bore to a wolf's. The
sharp, pointed shape, he had first noted, was
not only there, but also a keen wistfulness of
expression, an added intelligence, such as a
wolf on the scent might show.

Before the wayfarer had gained the nearest
place of shelter, he was convinced, by the
violent giddiness and nausea which grew upon
him, that he had, beyond doubt, been drugged,

if proof were needed of the truth of Wolf's alarm.

———

The traveller's after-wanderings took him into many lands, among countless new faces and associations, through not a few curious and some hazardous experiences.

But whether in sultry India or the lands of the old classics, looking on almond-eyed Celestials or flat-browed Esquimaux, there came always times when the face of Wolf, as he looked back through the gloom of the wood, returned vividly to his memory. It so forcibly impressed him, that, from time to time, he wrote letters in quest of Wolf. But never the faintest reply came back. Had the boy died? Or, worse, had he been foully dealt with? Had he paid, with a fearful penalty, for the rescue he had effected?

These misgivings often gave the traveller positive pain; and the sense of a great debt unpaid, rather increased than diminished, as often as he recalled the affair. Not unfrequently he peered into faces of a slightly similar cast, sailors about the quay, miners, workmen in the quarries he visited, half-expecting to recognize Wolf, under the guise of some bronzed, older face. But it never was Wolf.

As it neared one Christmas-tide, the traveller's face was turned towards home, after an absence from his native land, which had included several Christmases.

It was but the first day out that a slight scuffle and confusion on the deck attracted the traveller's notice.

"What was the row just now?" he inquired of a sailor.

"O! nothing to speak of," was the careless reply; "old Temper got his back up, and the captain had to knock him down handsome, that's all."

But, leaning over the scuttle leading to the steerage, a day or two after, the traveller was astonished to hear his own name shouted shrilly from below.

Twice over, it was repeated, and then, to the name was added, in a tone of mechanical repetition, that full address which, so long ago now, he had written out for Wolf. Then, again, as if in plaintive appeal, he heard his name called.

He was still standing, listening, when the ship's surgeon came up from below.

"See here, Doctor! who's that calling my name down there?" he inquired at once. His tone of interest convinced the surgeon that no idle curiosity impelled the question. He replied, courteously:

"A delirious sailor, whose own name I really cannot inform you of. He knows you, does he?"

"Truly, I should like to find out, by the captain's leave," was the response.

A little sulky the leave was, when granted, for the captain really felt somewhat aggrieved

that the troublesome sailor he had punished
for insubordination, should immediately take
occasion to fall sick of a brain fever, which
might partly be credited to a concussion of the
head when he fell under the blow, administered
in not unrighteous wrath.

" For whether you know him or not, sir,"
remarked the captain, hotly, "a peskier, sulkier
temper you never'll see in your life ! "

The face that lay in the sailor's bunk was
flushed with fever; the hair had already been
shaven close by the surgeon's orders, there
was nothing about the sick man that the
searching eyes scanning his prostrate length
could positively identify. His eyes looked up
with a dull, glazed stare; his hands wandered and groped.

They plucked at his coarse shirt, tore it
open, and clutched at something attached to
a strong string.

" Ah! what have we here? " said the surgeon, who, by the captain's orders had ac-

companied the traveller; "some souvenir from his sweetheart, probably."

But the traveller knew it well. It was a ring with a bloodstone set in it, in which had been cut part of a family crest.

"I must have this sailor well taken care of," said he, turning gravely to the Doctor. "Let us find the captain again. I want to tell both of you a little story."

Henceforth the sick man, during his illness lacked no care that could under the circumstances be afforded; for one who tended him felt that the opportunity had come to pay back the ransom risked on his own life — and he did not hold it cheap.

"All that a man hath, will he give for his life" — the words kept running in his head.

From the first, his influence on the sick man worked favorably. In the wild deliriums when the fever ran highest, the patient would obey from him commands, which the surgeon could only enforce by strength.

" It will be short and sharp," pronounced the surgeon; "and as to the end," he added more slowly, " I am very, very insecure."

But the friend whom the sailor had found, only resolved the more firmly that if effort could safe the life once ventured for his own, there should be no stint.

And so, by day and night, through the brief, hard fight, he was at the sailor's side, scarcely noting the passage, though it was a stormy and delayed one.

" Really, it is much in his favor that you have such a peculiar control over him," remarked the surgeon; "he acts as though he owned you master."

When the wildness and incoherence of the fever abated, a distressing restlessness came over the sick man. So plainly did it recall the disturbed night in the Australian inn, that the nurse was fain also, to recall for the second time, the old spell, and tell him stories like a child.

The droning voice, the rhythmic swing of the words, quieted the un-ease of body as before. For the first time a peaceful sleep came to the tired eyes. Hour after hour he slept, and the surgeon, feeling his faint pulse, fed carefully the springs of life that ran so low.

As the dawn broadened and brightened, the sick man stirred, though he lay as pallid as if lifeless on the pillow.

"Is it morning?" a whisper asked.

"Yes, it is morning," said the surgeon, in the tone of a man who has won a victory. "But swallow this now, and sleep a little longer."

It was morning; it was Christmas morning. One man had never been happy with such a peculiarly flavored happiness on any Christmas morning before. One must needs have known what it is to "help God find a life in the dark," in order to understand why that Christmas brought so delicious an elation to him. The land of home and kindred was in sight; he had accomplished, not unsuccessfully, long and toilsome journeying; but the thankfulness uppermost in his thoughts, after all, centre in the homeless, friendless youth, on whose recovery he had set his heart, for whose life he somehow felt responsible, as if it had been in the best sense a debt of honor.

So weak the convalescent lay, that, at first, everything seemed unreal and difficult of comprehension to him.

It only appeared like one part of the whole dream to be called "Wolf," as of old, and to return naturally to Wolf's submissive obedience to the one friend he had ever had. For poor Wolf never had made friends. Afterwards, in learning the little he had to tell, the gentleman could see that his moody temper and repellant manners would inevitably hedge him in as with a prickly barricade that few would care to break through, or be at the exertion of climbing over.

He held unreasoningly to his father as the only human ownership known to him, until that father died, killed in a drunken brawl. Then he had but one half-formed purpose, to seek the only friend he had left. ' Long ago, as the pencil marks blurred, he had learned by heart the traveller's written address. Where he had hidden the ring about his neck he continued to wear it from half-superstitious instinct. He had gone tossing about the world —now in a wayward mood giving up his plan, now resuming it; sometimes working as a miner, but oftenest as a sailor.

From that Christmas morning a new life began for the young fellow, whose career thus far had seemed without a plan, drifting merely at the mercy of the elements. For a while, the friend who assumed the responsibility of planning for him, was glad of his own exceeding natural wilfulness, for the nature he had to deal with was one that required determined mastership, in spite of its developing sense of gratitude, in spite of the hold acquired to begin with.

But years of patience are well paid for a true and sturdy manhood, such as that neglected boy was capable of.

One Christmas Eve the traveller called on his whilom Wolf—he never liked to have the old title given up—and they had a cosey chat together in Wolf's own special study. Across two open doors, by the reflection in a telltale mirror, showed a pretty tableau. It was Wolf's one little girl—and at that distance she reminded the traveller oddly of his long-ago pet Genevieve—hanging up her stocking beside the waiting crib.

"Please, mamma, after I am in, tell it to me again!" she pleaded, and then they heard the mother's soft voice, at intervals, as it threaded through "the old, old story," of the star, the manger, and the cross.

"And now, dear, what is the verse you learned?" asked the mother, as she finished.

And the child's shriller voice repeated, clearly:

"'Greater love hath no man than this, that a man lay down his life for his friends.'"

As the two strong men clasped hands, no words were spoken. In each heart there was gratitude to the other; in both hearts there was gratitude to the higher Love, whose constraining power we learn first sometimes from the love we bear each other.

"Now then!" uncle Brederode spoke up, in a brisk, business-like way, preventing comment on the last plum brought forth, "it is really my turn, at last; I won't be put off any longer!"

They listened to the deep, rich voice, as if it had never before sounded so pleasing.

CHAPTER XI.

PLUM THE SIXTH.

THIS is a story that has been told over by a certain mother to her children, many and many a time. It is the story they always liked the best, and begged to hear oftenest.

The mother used to make it quite a picture in their minds, about a slipper, that once stood, day after day, on the narrow ledge of a little window. It was a low, plain window, with many small, dull panes, but it looked out toward the west, and sometimes, when it reflected a yellow sunset, turned all

253

golden itself, and glowed so grandly, that it seemed to give a significance of royal state and honor to the simple brown house.

The young girl who used to live there (called Madge in those days), would imagine, at such times, as she came walking up the village street towards it, that it was indeed a palace illuminated for some splendid, glad festival to be kept within. But when the glow was gone, there it was the same sleepy, low-roofed dwelling again.

You would oftenest find this same Madge, not walking abroad and amusing herself with fancies, but sitting at work beside the slipper. It was a bronze kid, this slipper, and had, instead of a rosette, an odd French pattern wrought upon it in many-colored silks. But it did not stand on the narrow window-ledge for ornament's sake.

There were spools of thread, neatly sorted in it; scissors, a thimble, and such a pretty emery and wax-ball as Madge used to know how to make. The story of how it was, that the slipper turned thus into a work-basket, is this :

To begin with, it seems the Lyndes took their first boarder one summer when times were hard with them. It was a Miss Steadman.

She had heard of them through the Squire Albrey family, whom she knew. It did not take Madge long to fall deep in love with Miss Steadman. They gave up to her the parlor, which was the largest room in the house, and a sleeping-room which opened out of it, and by a few simple changes, a little ingenuity, Miss Steadman imparted to her little domain an air of grace and refinement.

She had a simple couch made, which could be wheeled about easily ; a few brackets and choice pictures were put up ; the rest of the furniture consisted chiefly of books and flowers, with the ferns and vines that Madge or Horace Albrey brought her from the woods.

In June, the large rose-tree blossomed gen-
erously, and she could pick its white buds
from one of her windows. Madge had trained
her morning-glory vines over another window.
The whole made a cool, quiet workroom for
the days when Miss Steadman was able to
write, and a soothing place to rest in on
those other — alas! too frequent — days, when
she had to lie still and suffering on the
chintz cushions of the couch.

The love and admiration which Madge felt
for Miss Steadman, taught her how to make
these days of pain easier to the invalid by
noiseless, unobtrusive ministrations, and Miss
Steadman liked to have the young girl with
her. She lent her books to Madge, she
taught her about many things in them, and
she taught her yet more by her own delicate
and well-bred way, and by the force of her
pure, sweet womanliness. She had studied
much. Madge found out after a while that
she could sing beautifully, and she even wrote
poems and stories.

Madge's love became almost reverent, she so felt the superiority of this being, far, far above herself. She hardly realized how deeply she did feel it till one Sunday night, when Miss Steadman, seeming stronger than usual, had been singing to them in the moonlight, on the porch. When she finished, Horace Albrey, who came every day to see her, and, in his frank, boyish way, adored her almost as much as Madge did, gave her a kiss as he very rarely did, and saying, "Good-night, Miss Rite," in a very subdued tone, went softly away. The others had gone in, and Miss Steadman was just drawing up her thick, white shawl to rise, when a sudden sob startled her.

"Why, Madge! what is the matter, dear?" said she, feeling for Madge's hand, and speaking in a startled tone.

Then Madge spoke out.

"Oh!" said she, "you make me feel so sorry and so ashamed? You can sing, and

you can write, and all — and there isn't one
single such splendid thing that I can do,
Miss Steadman. I don't seem to be good for
anything in particular, and I do *wish* I was!"

Her friend put one arm around Madge, and
drew the shawl over her, too, still holding
her hand. Then she asked Madge whether
she really thought any one intelligent being
had ever been made so that he or she could
not do some single thing well? "A wise man
hath said," Miss Steadman added, "'Every
human being is intended to have a character
of his own, to be what no other is, to do
what no other can do.' So I don't believe
you're left out, Madge, only may be you have
not just that you would choose given you to
do. And you must not blame yourself for
not having what you never had given you.
That is not your responsibility, you know.

"You remind me of another and an older
saying, 'We do not choose our own parts in
life, and have nothing to do with those parts:

our simple duty is confined to playing them well.' And do you know what you would choose, if you could, my child?"

Madge was not quite sure, after all.

"But *you* have not anything left to choose —you have everything already, I think," she said wistfully, nestling up to Miss Steadman.

"Ah, Madge!" answered Miss Steadman, half sportively, half sadly, "do you think I never mind being so weak as I am? that if I should tell you if I had my choice I believe I would like best to be like the railway trains, strong and quick, with muscles of iron and nerves of steel, and so always able, as well as ready, to fetch and carry for all sorts of people?"

Then Madge sat up and said eagerly:

"Why *I* could do that! *I* could fetch and carry!"

"So you could!" answered the lady, with quick sympathy, "surely dear! And, after all, aren't we each of us fetch-and-carriers? You know we cannot, any of us, create things; we can only fetch and carry what is already made; it is the skill in doing that which you admire. And you can make a really helpful business of it, if you try, Madge.

"As you say, you have strength and health, that is your capital, your stock in trade to begin upon. You envy me, dear, but I could almost envy you that."

Madge pressed Miss Steadman's hand lightly with her lips. She knew how frail and delicate she was, and how many were the days and nights of pain she passed.

"Now, then, let's plan it out nicely," resumed Miss Steadman, cheerfully, for she never dwelt upon her own ailments long. "In order to fetch and carry all you can, you must have quick eyes. Whenever you find helping thoughts in books you read or sermons you hear, save them up and remember them to carry again. Whenever you learn a new crotchet stitch or pretty bit of fancy work,

fetch that and carry it. Whenever you hear
a good story or a good joke, or a good deed,
save them to carry again. It will be like
adding up a column, now won't it? 'Set down
the aught and carry the one,' we used
to say in school. You will be saving and
passing on at the same time. Because
you are well and strong, carry some of your
strength to help the sick; because you are
young, carry to sad elder people news of happy
young doings. Even just going in to see them
will do it often. And I am sure you will find
so very much to save, that, as you fetch, you
will instinctively sort what you are to carry
again. You will sift out all that could be
hurtful, and only save the healthful things.
Never fetch and carry anything that will
hurt another or yourself."

Madge remembered that one of the neighbors was sick. Miss Steadman asked if she
had not heard how another was confined in-
doors continually by her household cares. And

they both agreed that plenty of fetching and carrying could be found to do in Madge's own home.

That talk helped Madge all her life. It showed her that there was no lack of useful work for her to do in the world, even though she had no voice for singing, did not like to write, and could not find out that any but homely talents had been committed to her.

Two Sundays after, Miss Steadman showed Madge a little book. The kind lady had made it herself, to cheer Madge on, and now that years have passed, the little book is treasured still.

That is how all these details came to be so well remembered.

The book opened at a comical pencil-sketch, representing a railway train at full speed, from whose every window, door and crevice, letters and packages of all sizes were spilling out along the track, while groups of people hurried with eager hands to pick them up.

On the title-page was printed, in official style:

FETCH AND CARRY R. R. REPORT.

The little book went on to chronicle how, per Fetch and Carry, the neighbor, too busy at home to go out, often had been brightened up when Madge ran in for half an hour's chat, and how she had sent a new receipt for breakfast cakes to Madge's mother. How the feeble neighbor had gladly received a handful of fresh morning glories every day. How an infirm old woman said it did her good to find the young folks hadn't forgotten her. How a kind remark made by one schoolmate of another, and carried by Madge, had averted a threatened misunderstanding. How glad Mrs. King was of Madge's offer to change her club book for her. How Saidie Penn learned to crotchet a summer hood for her mother's birthday. How Mrs. Lynde, Madge's mother, said that it made all the difference in the house, if you had somebody to go out among people, and bring in something fresh and bright. How a certain Miss Marguerite Steadman received regularly fresh ferns and bouquets for her room, cool glasses of water when her head ached, and ready doing of errands. How a whole Saturday afternoon had been spent in taking care of the busy neighbor's children, that the tired mother might have a chance to take a little air.

How Johnnie had been comforted, in composing his composition, by a good illustration that his elder sister remembered and repeated to him. How Bessie and her dollies considered Madge, in all their varied experiences, a never-failing refuge.

"The Fetch and Carry R. R.," winds up the little book, " declares a daily dividend of ninety-nine per cent."

"I thought I might say that," said Miss Rite, as Madge was learning to call her, "because you have looked so happy these two weeks, dear little Fetch-and-Carrier."

Seeing that Madge grew more and more in earnest in her work, she oftener than any other applied to her the name of "Little Fetch-and-Carrier."

"Keep on, dear," she would say, "God will give you more and more to fetch, and more and more to carry, and strength enough for all."

But the summer came swiftly to an end, and Miss Rite had staid as long as she could. The writing, she had sought this quiet place to finish, was done. She packed unwillingly, left some books and keep-sakes in Madge's hands, and kissed her good-by. She looked tenderly, almost compassionately, at Madge.

She knew that the family had no easy time to live, and wished that she could help them without offending their pride and reserve. "If I have left anything, keep it," she said, leaning out of the car window. "Keep up our Fetch and Carry, and expect me back next summer, Madge."

She never came. By another summer her wish had come true; she was one among the angels who excel in strength.

Horace walked home with Madge that afternoon, in late September, after they had said good-by to Miss Rite, and they walked awhile in the garden, which looked empty enough, having given its last flowers to Miss Rite on her departing. When Horace had taken the little bundle destined for his mother, and gone, Madge remembered to wonder if, by chance, Miss Rite had left anything. Feeling no heart for any sort of fetching and carrying just then, she turned sadly to the deserted rooms. One by one she opened all the drawers, and looked in. A perfume lingered about them, nothing more.

A morsel of paper littered the floor.

As she stooped to pick it up, mechanically,

something blue caught her eye, glistening mischievously in a shady corner, under the bed. It was that very slipper. Madge picked it up tenderly, half-smiling and half-sighing, as she looked at the pattern wrought on the slipper in blue and purple and gold silks. She had always thought these slippers wonderful, and had regarded them with such frequent, admiring looks that Miss Rite had said, one day, " I see you like my pretty slippers. They came over the water to me. Is not the bunch of heart's-ease natural ? "

" I never saw anything so pretty," Madge answered, and then added, timidly, " is it very hard to learn embroidery, Miss Rite? I always wanted to learn, and if I once could do anything so nice as that bunch of pansies, or heart's-ease, as you call it, I can't think but I should be as happy as a painter, when he paints flowers."

" Sure enough! it is much the same thing," Miss Rite answered. " The French call embroidery painting with the needle. I can show you a little about embroidery, if you would like to learn so much; and I don't doubt you will get to the pansies yet; my favorite flower, by the way."

Madge was, beyond measure, grateful for the teaching which, after this, Miss Rite gave her in embroidery, and she tried her very best to learn. From that time Miss Rite's favorite vase was never left empty of pansies, so long as they were obtainable; and, in their season, Miss Rite would often wake in the morning to find the first thing her eyes rested on, the dainty slippers, standing by her bed, filled with fresh, wide-awake pansies. Before she was dressed there would be, perhaps, a small, smothered rap at her door, and. upon her "Come," little Bessie would laboriously turn the knob, and enter.

"Did you find 'em?" she would ask. "Madge and me picked 'em, and she came in on tip-toe, when you were asleep."

"I did find them, little Bessie," Miss Rite
would reply, "and they made me think of
the shoe-full of children that the Old Woman
had so many of she didn't know what to do.
Come and look at the pansies, while I braid
my hair, and let's name them. Don't you see
they look just like faces, children's faces?"

They would have a merry time choosing
names for the yellow pansies, which Bessie
said were like new, yellow chickies, the purple pansies, and the half-and-half pansies; then
Miss Rite would fasten a bunch at her throat
and let Bessie lead her gaily in to breakfast.

One morning, however, only one of the
slippers could be found. Bessie heard the
inquiry made about it with a look of dismay;
and, by and by, a sobbing little culprit
entered Miss Rite's room, to tell the sad story
of the missing slipper. It was rather incohe-
rent, but Miss Rite made out, that, yesterday
afternoon, when she had been at the Albrey's
to tea, Bessie had bethought herself to fill

the slipper with flowers, as Madge did.
"They'll keep cool over night, if I leave 'em
out here," reasoned the child, as she snipped
off her one own rose, which had just blossomed, and proudly placed it in the slipper.
"I want Miss Rite to have my rose, and I
can put in dandelions all 'round it."

Having arranged it to her satisfaction, Bessie
bestowed the slipper in her beloved play-house,
and then forgot all about it till morning.
Hurrying to bring it from the play-house
shelf, what was her horror to find it gone.
There was a row of scattered dandelions, but
no slipper. The dog next door was discovered
gnawing something that bore a faint resemblance to a slipper, during the day. Poor
little Bess! she went about looking heart-
broken for half the day, which was as long
as any state of mind could last with such a
baby. "I didn't 'spect to be so naughty, I
truly didn't!" she wept, remorsefully; and
Miss Rite had comforted and forgiven her.

It was at the remembrance of these things that Madge smiled and sighed as she held the slipper for a moment. But, at the end of the moment, she was sure she heard Bessie crying, somewhere. She pushed the scrap of paper — which she had seen immediately to be only half of a quotation in Miss Rite's hand-writing, not making sense by itself — into the furthest corner of the slipper, and laid it gently away in her best drawer. I'm not sure but a tear went in with it before she hurried off to see what had happened to Bessie.

It was not until after she had grown too accustomed to the absence of her friend to cry about it, that this "odd notion," as her mother called it, occurred to her. She lined the slipper, still leaving the useless bit of paper, which she had picked up on the day of Miss Rite's departure, just where it was — perhaps she was a trifle sentimental about it, and no harm if she was — and fitted it all up like this. She liked to have it beside her when she sat long hours sewing, to remind her of that happy summer and sweet Miss Rite, who was safe in heaven now as Horace Albrey's mother had told her.

She had need to hoard all the past sunshine to be happy in, for things present were looking gloomy when winter came on.

Mr. Lynde's business had not prospered well. The new baby was a sickly little fellow, and the mother far from strong.

Madge gave up her school, and seemed all at once to change from girl to woman. She sewed, and planned, and economized, and was busy fetching and carrying from morning till night.

But still it was not so very hard till Mr. Lynde, the father, fell ill. Even after the dread and danger of his long sickness were over, there was still a slow recovery, fickle and protracted.

Then it was that Madge became closer

crony than ever of her slipper. She had
become, by faithful practice, quite skilful in
embroidery, and she took in such work to do,
feeling almost as though she had found her
one talent, she could do it so easily and suc-
cessfully. Still, if, at times, she could not
get embroidery to do, she was thankful for
the aprons and petticoats that Mrs. Wendell,
the doctor's wife, gave her to make for the
children. So busy did Madge become with
needle-work that you scarcely saw her apart
from the slipper. Her father, as he lay
watching her, would sportively call her the
real Old Woman who lived in a shoe. He
did not realize, for she would not have let
him, on any account, what a fight for cheerful courage and patient heart she had to
make as she sat stitching until it was too
dark to see, even by the lingering light of
the west window, day after day.

Horace Albrey, who had never given up
coming familiarly to the house since he had

fallen into the habit during Miss Rite's stay there, noticed, when he would tap on the pane and leave a message from his mother about her work, that she was looking pale and tired. He made all the more fun and joked about the shoe and the Old Woman — that was his way.

And she always laughed back, and gave him some ready rejoinder — that was her way. But Horace and his dog, as they went away, walked more and more slowly over the bridge.

" If I dared," said Horace, " but she's proud if she is still; would you, Karl ? "

Karl looked up and yawned, as if to say: " I give it up, master."

The next day was a stormy one. Madge could not sew as usual, because her father was worse, and the baby very fretful. The shoe waited lonely on the sill. Horace, coming up to the window, as usual, found no little Old Woman there. He slipped something into the shoe and ran fast over the bridge towards home, racing with Karl. It was only a bunch of white grapes that Madge found in the slipper, but that chanced to suit the sick man's capricious taste, and the whole disturbed household machinery seemed to move easier for it.

The audacious Horace came just the same next day, and when Madge told him about the grapes, with grateful emphasis, he only declared coolly that it was a capital idea, he might have thought of it himself, and now that she had put it into his head, of course —

From that time there was no end to the distortions that poor slipper had to undergo, with papers of chocolate, oranges, bananas and sometimes the latest book or monthly.

But the prettiest part of the story is the Christmas part, that which tells how Madge found the other half of that torn quotation she had picked up from the floor on the day when she had said good-by to Miss Rite.

Christmas was near at hand, and though Madge and her people had always needed to be careful and saving, they had never been so pinched with poverty before.

They missed the strong arm of the bread-winner, and how could Madge's little earnings be sufficient to pay the doctor's bill, and buy the flour, and keep them all in shoes, and supply the strengthening food her father needed? For all that, they grieved just as much when the baby died as if they had plenty and to spare to bring it up with. They had always been quiet, thrifty people, and no one realized at all the straits to which they were reduced. The Albreys had all gone to the city to spend Christmas, and the only piece of work which Madge had on hand was one wanted by Mrs. Albrey for a Christmas gift. It was a silk lambrequin, embroidered with a single golden wheat sheaf, and bunches of pansies. It could not be done before Mrs. Albrey left, because of the baby's death;

but Madge had promised to finish it and send it in season, and she was sitting up nights to keep her promise. As the pansies grew under her light, quick fingers, how many thoughts sweet, and bitter, were tangled with the floss. Here she was working the bunch of Miss Rite's pansies. Dear Miss Rite! it was all owing to her, but she wasn't here to see. And if she had been, she would have seen also how discouraged and harassed Madge felt in spite of herself at not being able to make a merry Christmas for the children, at the memory of those hopeless-looking debts, at the sight of her father's feeble looks, and her mother's thin, sad face. "What a satire it seems, to be working heart's-ease!" thought Madge wearily one night.

She was on the very last flower now, and the pretty thing must go to-morrow or her promise would be broken. But the purple floss fell short, to her dismay; she had been sure there would be enough. It was after

midnight, and poor Madge knew, without looking, that she had actually not enough money
in her purse to buy the skein of purple floss,
even if she could match it in the morning.

"But how can I disappoint kind Mrs.
Albrey?" thought Madge.

In her desperation, it suddenly occurred to
her, as her eye fell on the slipper with its
pansy pattern, to feel away into the toe and
try if she could not possibly find and pick
out the little purple silk she would need to
finish with. Turning its contents into her lap,
she hastily ripped out the lining, and brought
out with it, as she gave the slipper a gentle
shake, two bits of white paper rolled up small.
How the hot blood rushed to her pale face
as she unfolded them! That half of a quotation she had placed there, she remembered
perfectly well; but the other not only completed the sense of the line, it held a bank-
note, whose image and superscription wavered
and trembled before Madge's astonished eyes.

Mechanically she fitted the ragged edges of the torn bits of paper together, and now it read, clear and coherent:

"It chanced; Eternal God that chance did guide."

When Madge showed this bit of mosaic work to her father in the morning, and told him the whole story, he said with a trembling voice:

"This is a pretty good lesson to us, daughter, to remember that when we can't make sense of anything, Providence has surely got the other half somewhere."

How long Madge sat and thought over the slipper and the note she held in her hand, that night, she never knew. She was putting everything together and accounting for it all. She remembered Miss Rite's parting words and significant look. She remembered a half-finished proffer that Miss Rite had begun to the house-mother the morning of her departure, and then had left incomplete with a blush.

She guessed that Miss Rite had seen that summer how really poor they were, but had been too delicate herself not to see also just how sensitive they were, too, and had found that she could not offer them help directly. So, at the very last moment, probably, she had hastily wrapped up this bank-bill in half a stray bit of paper, pushed it into the very toest part of the slipper, and left the familiar pansies to announce themselves. She might well be sure that her devoted lover Madge would cherish and keep the slipper for its associations, and she probably had no thought that the money could remain undiscovered so long.

Ah! but we know Who had kept it there till just the time when it was needed most!

It would have done Miss Rite good to know what a help, in their emergency, her bank-bill proved to the Lyndes, and what a different Christmas it made for all of them. Madge could not rest until the whole story was known to Mrs. Albrey, who, having known her friend so well, could put all Madge's scruples to rest, by saying:

"My dear, you need not hesitate to use it, in the least, for that is just like Rite Steadman, her very impulsive, generous, uncalculating way. She was always doing things that nobody else would have thought of, in ways that nobody else would have dared to try, and it certainly did seem as though Providence encouraged her in it."

The children, who know all this by heart, know also that, after this Christmas Day, with its gift, which seemed to come from heaven, more placid times passed over the little brown country house. Though the Albreys removed to the city, and were gradually lost sight of, the children have heard how kind all the old neighbors were to the Lyndes; and they can guess that this friendly help of theirs made part of the dividends from Madge's Fetch and Carry. Furthermore, it is known to the children that, once upon a time, a love-note was found by Madge — now a woman grown — in her slipper, and all that came of that they are familiar with. And they think it, these children, as good as a sermon to go and look at the same faded slipper, laid away and kept with great care, at some times when they are worried, or anxious, or pinched for money.

For the Madge of this story has never, to the present day, been rich, and is not now strong and well as she was in the days when she founded the Fetch and Carry, with dear Miss Rite's help.

But her children intend to continue for her the running of the Fetch and Carry. It has always paid increasing dividends.

Though Miss Rite's more elaborate books have had a wider circulation, Madge's children would not be willing to exchange for any one of them the unpretentious first Report of this same Fetch and Carry. And they would fain hope, that, through them, it may still go on busily and modestly, helping more and more people who need its lesson and its encouragement, or, who need, as we all do sometimes, to be fetched for and carried.

As uncle Brederode stopped reading, he looked up with a quiet smile at Rite's pink cheek.

"And what would you say, Miss Rite," he asked, slowly, "if I should tell you that I know this Mr. Horace Albrey well? That we have travelled together for months at a time?

"That, furthermore, he being about to settle down and make a home in this country, with his wife, and the children, who have been studying abroad, I have an appointment to examine the Audrey place with him, no later than next Monday?"

"Why, I should say, sir," replied Rite,

while her mother bent forward, flushing almost as pink as Rite in her surprise, "that it would be almost like having a story-book hero appear in flesh and blood, for me actually to meet this hero of mother's stories."

"Well, well," smiled her questioner, "we shall see presently.

"But it will not do now to keep the children waiting. Is it your plum, Ronald?"

For Ronald was fidgetting in evident impatience.

"I want Dolly to have it," declared Ronald, stoutly, "but we've asked Miss Maudie to read it aloud, because we can't. I know it's aunt Moneywort's, though."

CHAPTER XII.

SOMEHOW your aunt Moneywort is not the kind that ever gets rid of things. So, though she feebly protested when cousin Red asked her for this contribution to our very remarkable Pie, she knew that the nature of things was against her.

"How absurd for me to go and write out a long story all about myself!" she exclaimed.

"Now, Aunt Moneywort," coaxed cousin Red, "you know you haven't it in your

285

heart to spoil the baking of this Pie I've set my affections on; no, nor even to discourage the mixing of it, by saving out any of the spice you might put in."

And aunt Moneywort knew she hadn't.

But she said to herself, "Then I will tell the story, not of myself, but of my bag. Is not aunt Moneywort said in the family to be known by her bag? Let her then respectfully retire behind the Bag itself.

The old Bag has been a great traveller, and no wonder that after many years of hard service, it should look bulgy and collapsed at once.

But it was fresher than it now is when aunt Moneywort one afternoon arrived with it at the sister's house which she called home.

She had been down in Bangor helping through Annette's wedding, and had a great deal to gossip about with her sisters, who had all assembled to meet her, while she unpacked her bag.

They were visiting together, and laughing and talking while they discussed all the news, when in came one of those dreadful yellow envelopes. There was no help for it; aunt Moneywort and all the sisters, sobered immediately, had to set to work and cram the old bag again till it stood as fat as ever, with the usual slip-shod and one-sided grin where it could not possibly be shut together.

"And O! your papers!" exclaimed one sister, after the bag was supposed to be full. "Of course you'll take them, since you're going right to the spot?"

"Of course!" replied aunt Moneywort, with emphasis. "I'm so glad you thought of them, because I should have been obliged to go again, otherwise. And my bank book, too! I must have the interest put on."

So the precious papers were deposited in the safest pocket, with aunt Moneywort's purse, thimble and scissors, a sandwich or two, and, as they all supposed, her invaluable, her in-

separable eye-glasses. But poor aunt Moneywort, when, seated breathless in the car, she
needed the glasses to count out the change,
fidgetted over the bag in vain.   •

"They must be here!" she declared sternly,
as she catechised the bag with severity.

"No, no, no! I cannot tell a lie!" was
the only answer from every pocket and corner, when she had finished her investigations.

Upon which bereaved aunt Moneywort could
only shut her near-sighted eyes resignedly, and
lay back in despair.

But it was not that over which aunt Moneywort was looking so grave. O, no! but the
baby was sick — sister Sue's beautiful baby —
and the swift express train could scarcely carry
her fast enough.

At the door of sister Sue's house baby's
elder sister met her tearfully; even to welcome *her* the mother would not leave her
baby.

"It is such a relief to see you, auntie,"

said baby's sister; "give me the blessed bag, and go to mother, please."

At the baby's side, his mother lifted her haggard face and dropped almost fainting against aunt Moneywort.

Yes, the poor, beautiful baby was very sick. He looked almost like death as he lay in his crib. The auntie slipped away to pull her warm wrapper and noiseless slippers from the bag, and put them on; then, almost forcing the worn-out mother to rest, took up her watch beside the baby.

The house was painfully still; it was very dull for wee Maisie, who was almost a baby herself. Nobody minded her to-day, and she was used to being minded. Bridget had been amusing her in the play-room, but somebody had called Bridget, and she had been left quite alone this long while. Maisie went wandering about the house. They said she mustn't go where baby was — poor baby, he was so sick, Bridget said.

The sitting-room was shut up, the parlor was cold, the dining-room looked dusty, mamma's plants were all drying up in the bay window. Maisie watered them so zealously that the water ran all over the carpet.

Then she sighed and wished there were more to do, and wandered restlessly into the spare room. O! whose pretty bag was that? Maisie knew — she had every reason to know. Auntie always brought this bag when she came, and there was pretty sure to be something specially for Maisie in it, to the delight of that small maid.

Maybe there would be a new hat for her dolly, or a picture-book, or a ribbon, or a paper of sweets. Maisie quite adored this bag. She thought it grand to go riding round with it like auntie. Once she shut up her kitten in this bag and forget all about it, and auntie carried it off, not knowing what she was doing, until the kitten jumped out

in her face, on the cars. Yes, Maisie's restless fingers always itched to try experiments
with that bag. And now it came over her
what a fine thing it would be to play lady
with the bag, and pretend she was aunt Moneywort going off in the cars. It would be such
a nice play she thought.

Maisie took down her own small hat and
cloak, and put them on clumsily.

There was nobody to notice when she
slipped out of the door and round the corner
with the bag on her arm. Nobody in the
house had any thought just then except for
the suffering baby.

When at last they did realize that Maisie was
not to be found in the house, nobody thought
to miss the bag also. The sick child was
mercifully easier after a frightful spasm, his
exhausted mother had fallen into a light doze
on the couch, and aunt Moneywort was keeping watch over both, when the door softly un-
closed, and a face looked in with such a

frightened pallor on it, that aunt Moneywort stepped quickly out to see what could be this new trouble.

At that moment the sharp clang of the fire-alarm sounded. For this they none of them spared a thought.

Maisie! darling, ignorant little Maisie, where was she? The servants, the neighbors, Maisie's father, hastened in all likely directions to seek the stray child; aunt Moneywort and her niece could only stay to care for the sick, and control themselves into outward composure for the over-wrought mother's sake.

The streets were noisy, yet, to the suspense in which they waited in that hushed, shaded room at nightfall, all were strangely deadened.

"Is there no news of her?" one of the watchers would steal out to ask at every footfall, as the evening dragged on.

"None, Miss," the servant answered, as they returned unsuccessfully. "And O, Miss! there's

a great fire, only a few squares away. See,
it's awful!'"

Yet, still, the one engrossing anguish of fear
and dread about the lost pet kept them from
a thought of actual apprehension with regard
to the fire. When the sense of such danger
did come, it was with a sudden shock.

The father, seeking his home, in the forlorn hope that tidings of Maisie might wait
him there, saw with horror the resistless ap-
proach of the flames. No time was to be
lost. With every care possible the sick child
and his mother were taken to the nearest
place of safety, then the rest of the family
worked, as if for their lives, to pack and make
ready for removal what valuables could be
saved.

The next morning's light found an ashen
blank where last night the house had stood.

It was a terrible, unnatural night.

While the men and horses fought the fierce
fire that seemed as if it would swallow half

the city in its unsated appetite, a few white-faced women fought for the baby's flickering life, in the strange house that had opened to shelter them, poor refugees that they had become!

The baby's mother had no time to miss Maisie. "This will be my baby's death!" was her one thought.

The baby's father, almost distracted between the child who seemed dying, the lost home, and the missing Maisie, was out seeking wildly all that weird night till day-break.

With the morning came so much comfort as this. Aunt Moneywort had watched by too many sick-beds not to be able to trust her own judgment; and, to her eyes, the baby was really better, miraculous as it seemed after the hazardous night.

The little body that had been so tortured lay quieter; the breathing was more even.

"Better! he is better, darling!" she whispered to the baby's mother, and the words strengthened the worn woman.

"O! I can do anything! I can bear anything now!" she whispered back, and really smiled again as she spoke.

"Can you even take care of him for an hour without me, dear?" asked aunt Moneywort, steadily.

"O yes!" said the mother, not thinking anything strange after the strange night.

So aunt Moneywort only added, "Do not leave him till I come back, dear," and softly went away.

She had a feeling somehow that nobody but herself could find Maisie.

"And Maisie must be found! Maisie must be found!" she repeated within herself, firmly.

She tied on the first bonnet that came to her hand, without wondering whose it was, she pinned on somebody's shawl without leave.

A face that she scarcely knew, for that of Maisie's papa, it was so wan and deathly, came up behind her. He looked at her vacantly. "Where are you going?" he said, in an apathetic tone.

Aunt Moneywort is strong and tall. She half-lifted her brother to the nearest lounge, and covered him with a travelling-rug, speaking as one whom it will do no good to resist.

"I am going to find Maisie. Lie here and lie still. You have got your baby back, and I believe that you are going to have Maisie back, too."

On her way out she sent some one — she was not very clear who it was — to get a glass of cordial for the worn-out man, who was too thoroughly spent to stir from the position in which she had placed him.

Swiftly, swiftly through the smoky air strode aunt Moneywort, thinking fast and saying half aloud, "Maisie! Maisie! Maisie!"

She hurried past the blackened walls of a half-burnt church. A gay toy horse lay across the very threshold. A group of shivering, homeless people huddled together within. Strange piles of goods were stacked in the little square.

She could scarcely recognize at first the altered spot whence she had fled last night. She scooped up a handful of the yet hot ashes, thinking that she would be tempted to save them, if she knew that those particular ones represented the relics of her faithful old bag.

"But it is gone," she thought; "strange that I could have forgotten it last night, and O! my papers! my papers!"

Aunt Moneywort groaned. It was the first chance she had had to realize her loss, and all it involved.

It was the dearest wish of aunt Money-wort's heart to have a little house of her own; it had been the dream of years.

She had several sisters, all whole-hearted, affectionate and hospitable, who were glad to have her with them for any length of time.

But aunt Moneywort wanted a place all hers, where, in her turn, she could welcome nieces, nephews and all, keep a cat and a cactus, and give an occasional tea-party, when she was at home long enough.

She had been saving up for years, to this end, and last year she had had a bequest left her, which, with the sale of the pasture-land grandpa had willed to her years ago, and the carefully hoarded bank-money, made her feel that, by the spring, she might consider herself rich enough to buy a snug, small house, in Out-and-Out Street, of which she had the refusal.

Now it had not been easy to find a purchaser for the land willed to aunt Moneywort by her grandfather, years ago; and when, at last, in the course of the carpet-bag's wanderings up and down the earth, a Mr. Ezra Amidowne was discovered, willing to pay the fair though modest sum for it, which counted so much to aunt Moneywort, he died suddenly, before the whole sum had been paid in.

His heirs did not want the property, and objected that the price asked for it, was too high. They declared that the amount claimed by aunt Moneywort as due, should only be paid on her producing the papers to prove that Ezra Amidowne had legally agreed to give the price which she stated.

Of course aunt Moneywort, when she packed the papers in the bag, had been all ready to do so; but if now the papers were gone — poor aunt Moneywort!

She shut her teeth together, and tried to put all thoughts of that bag out of her mind.

"Maisie, Maisie, that is the one thing I must think of now!" she said. "What might not have happened to the poor, bewildered child during that fearful night?" Aunt Moneywort shuddered and sickened to think of all the dangers to which she might have been

exposed, but she only walked on faster. Whenever she came upon groups of homeless people, or heaps of ruined goods, wherever a
child's voice was heard, there she searched
and questioned, but in vain.

The city began to rouse more thoroughly,
the streets to grow more thronged. No
one stared at aunt Moneywort; there were
plenty of scared-looking, oddly-clothed people
in the streets that morning.

By and by, some one addressed her.

"Is this the way to the depot, the Rey-
nardville depot, ma'am?"

There was a tremulous tone of trouble in
the voice of the young girl who asked this
question, that called Aunt Moneywort to herself.

"You have taken the wrong turn, I think,"
she answered, "but it is no wonder you
were confused. I will show you, it is not
far."

"After all, what does it matter which way

Aunt Moneywort is astonished.

I go, " she thought, "when I have no clue where to look?"

"You're very kind," said the girl at her side. "You see, my uncle that I came to visit, he's burnt out — and I was so dreadfully frightened — and we lost each other in the crowd — and if I could only get home to my mother!"

"O dear!" grumbled foolish aunt Moneywort. "Now I shall have to stay long enough to see this girl safe on her train under the conductor's care. So much time lost!"

Yes, the foolish woman! How ashamed she was afterwards for that thought!

"Your train leaves in ten minutes," she said, as they entered the depot; "have you money to get your ticket? Come into the ladies' room, and I —"

Aunt Moneywort stopped and gasped.

There were only three or four women in the ladies' room, waiting for the early train.

There was a little heap on the hard lounge,

with the face turned away, and yellow, tumbled curls flying loose. She had a bag pressed close up to her breast, a bag that really seemed to wink at aunt Moneywort across the waiting room.

For a steady, experienced woman like aunt Moneywort, it was not very creditable to get that young girl left, was it? Aunt Moneywort, the traveller of the family, who never missed a train, and had even been to South America. But considering, that, upon examination, the frightened girl discovered that she had not a penny about her, and that aunt Moneywort's purse and all her precious papers lay untouched in the bag, it may have been just as well.

Maisie, feeling herself squeezed, as if with a hug that would never let go, opened her eyes composedly, and remarked, with a critical air: "What you got your bonnet on wrong side 'fore for, auntie?"

Then, being wider awake, she sat up in her

aunt's arms and, added, in the midst of a yawn, half frightened away, "What you a-cryin' for, cryin' *tears*, auntie?"

"Auntie stopped "cryin' tears" as soon as she conveniently could, and, having arranged for the young traveller who had guided her to Maisie just as straight as an angel could have done, she hurried the child and the blessed bag away in a hack — not home, indeed — ah! the poor, pretty home that Maisie would never see again! — but to the loving arms that could ignore the loss of worldly wealth while they clasped this recovered treasure.

Dear, foolish little Maisie! it is doubtful how much she understood about it all. She told them how she had thought it would be nice to play go a-travelling just like aunt Moneywort, with her big, pretty bag. It took her a good while to get where the cars were, she said, and once some horses most stepped on her, and once she dropped the bag. By and by she saw some other people walking along with bags and *she* went and *they* went, and they all came to where the cars go!

"Then I was drefful tired," said Maisie, "and I tried to open the bag, but 'twas locked, and I thought I'd rest my shoes; my shoes were so — so sore on the bottom of 'em, you know. And that's all.

"But have I been far yet? Is this far off? Have they got any meat and potatoes here?" Maisie evidently had an idea that she had been "travelling like auntie" all this time.

Though thus suddenly they found themselves homeless and poor, that burned-out family felt that they had enough to keep a Thanksgiving Day for.

Aunt Moneywort privately hugged her bag. Why! don't you see? there was a home in it! It stood for the cat, and the cactus, and the place of her own; and, better than all, for a home that could be offered to sister Sue, the baby that was given back, little Maisie and all of them, until Maisie's father could have time to look about him and find another place. She did not put off taking the house in Out-and-out street till spring, but fitted it up simply at once, and was so proud and glad in playing hostess in the real home she had so long coveted, that, few presents as they could afford to give among themselves, that first Christmas there seemed the happiest of her life.

One of the sisters borrowed the bag, on pretense of needing it for a day's journey.

Sure enough, it went on a day's journey, but only to be passed round among the sisters, who all dropped something in it; and back it came on Christmas morning with such a load of loving, helpful Christmas presents in it, just what aunt Moneywort, new in housekeeping, most needed, that that happy woman could only relieve her feeling by dashing into the kitchen and cooking up panfuls of what Maisie called "*tracks.*" Maisie used to take great delight in watching all aunt Moneywort's cooking; and, when the moulding-board was full of tea-biscuits, or cookies, which the cook proceeded to mark one by one with a floury fork, Maisie would say, "You're making just like bird tracks in the snow, auntie!"

From this, Maisie took up a funny little fashion of her own, of asking, when she was hungry, "Please one of your tracks, auntie?"

Aunt Moneywort knew plenty of people who would be even more glad than Maisie was to get such "tracks" as these — plenty of children who were homeless as well as hungry to-day.

So, because she really could not help it, her heart was so full of Christmas joy and Thanksgiving gratitude, she filled the bag full, and took it around with her among such people all the rest of the day, trying to cheer them up, and to find something to do for them.

A very busy bag that one continued to be, as well after the day when Maisie set out to go travelling with it, as before, until finally even aunt Moneywort's relatives observed that its labors were becoming too much for its constitution, and Lou embroidered a gorgeous substitute, for aunt Moneywort's birthday present. She presented this with a speech so full of flattery that aunt Moneywort dropped her eye-glasses and smashed them in her embarrassment. Who could unblushingly endure being called "the angel with the carpet-bag"?

By this time even the most distant family relatives have grown used to the association of Lou's gold and maroon bag, bearing the flying angel for a centre-piece, with the appearance of aunt Moneywort. It is now as inseparable from her, in her frequent journeys, as the old bag was in its day. But that faithful former companion is hung up tenderly in a safe place, and keeps house for aunt Moneywort when she is gone from home.

Nor is its day of usefulness over, for it is trusted to hold valued old letters, with many a story and association linked to their fast yellowing pages.

And sometime Maisie shall have the bag for a Christmas present, to remember her adventure by.

CHAPTER XIII.

THE WARMED-OVER PIE.

"IS that all?"

"Can't we have any more?"

"Was there ever such a feast of plums!"

Such ejaculations· followed each other, as the reading ended.

"But what a pity," said one of aunt Moneywort's nieces, regretfully, "that poor, dear aunt Moneywort could not be here to enjoy all these goodies with us!"

"Yes; it's hard to be reconciled to that

luckless sprained ankle of hers," assented Miss Maudie.

"Let's make it up to her," spoke cousin Red, brightly. "Let's pack the splendid Pie once more, and fill up all the cracks with sugar-plums — for our blessed aunt Moneywort likes sugar-plums just as well as any girl — and pass the whole thing on to her to-morrow by express. I know just how much comfort she'll take in the warmed-over Pie."

"And I'd like to tuck in a Christmas token at the same time," said a voice.

"And I!"

"And I!" added other people, warmly.

But Mr. Sylverner interrupted.

"Before we leave our delectable Pie," said he, "I move an emphatic vote of thanks to the successful cook, and three hearty cheers for the plums, the like of which I never expect to taste again!"

The ceremonies thus indicated were at once performed, amid cousin Red's laughing disclaimers, and the pushing back of chairs, as the party around the table broke up into duos and trios, discussing the various plums.

Maud's "particular friend" lingered as if waiting for her, but she was so long in replacing, with great precision, the contents of the Pie, and then in receiving certain packets which were brought her at once to be added thereto, that he turned away with Louise Swallow, and there was nobody left to wonder why, of all things that could be mixed with the seasoning of the "warmed-over Pie," Maud should have dropped in a tear or two.

When she reappeared in the parlors, however, the fair face seemed as smiling as ever, and no one of the cordial, unaffected ways which made her so dear to all her kindred was missing, as she helped on her young guests through all the festivities of glad Christmas Eve.

The Christmas Pie had hardly been for half an hour left to itself in its restored perfection, when some one returned to the dimly lighted room. The intruder had a small, flat parcel in his hand, and he appeared to wish to find a place for it in the very bowels of the Pie.

" Ha!" he exclaimed to himself suddenly, in the midst of his careful rummaging.

The vacant room seemed to listen as if to hear what he had found that should cause his ejaculation; but he said no more, and the Pie was left solitary again.

By and by a child stole in on tip-toe, and dropped a pet toy into the Pie.

The Pie was going to auntie full of presents from them all; she had heard the bigger people say so. Poor, sick auntie should have her newest, nicest plaything; then, with a heart beating fast as she peered furtively among the shadows of the room, the child hurried back to the lights and company.

Later, when the music and charades were over, when the children had hung up their stockings, and good-nights had sounded on the stairs, Maud herself came back to the dining-room, and showed, as she turned up the gas, an anxious, troubled face. She smiled as she noted how much fuller the Pie had grown, and how small space, after all, would be left in it for sugar-plums.

But this diverted only for a moment her perturbed search for something which evidently she did not succeed in finding in the Pie, and the perplexity deepened in her face.

"What is it, Maud?" asked a voice behind her, that made her start.

"I have lost it," she replied, mournfully. "I have certainly lost grandma's topaz ring. How careless I must have been not to remember that it is much too large for my finger! But what will papa say to me if I cannot find it?"

"Is that all you have lost?" questioned Maud's "particular friend," very gently and gravely. "Now I have missed something much more valuable. If I could give you

back the ring, could you give me back something — your trust in me, Maud?"

She saw him ⸃ hold up the antique topaz,
but it seemed to dance, yellow and unsteady,
before her misty eyes, like a torch in the rain.

"You know you seemed" — she tried to
speak proudly, but her voice was very low.

"I know I seemed to avoid you, and to
court Miss Louise's society; but if I tell you
that it was only because of a Christmas mystery undertaken for your sake, cannot Mistress
Agatha's faithless little descendant 'trust me
true,' say till to-morrow?"

The two drew close together, and once
more troth and trust for a life-time were plighted
over Mistress Agatha's ring.

Later still the stockings, puffed out in all
manner of queer shapes, hung in their places
unwatched. The rustling and laughing from
the chambers where the girls slept, three in
a bed, had gradually ceased.

Rite, in her place beside Maud, who had

Nettie Periwinkle had a finger in the Pie

318

insisted that she should stay all night with the rest of the girls, could not sleep for thinking of what it would be to meet the knight and friend of her mother's girlhood. What would he look like? Would he buy the old Audrey place, called by the name so like his own, and restore it to its old luxury.

And what would be the next thing, then, for themselves?

"If we could only go back to the country!" thought Rite.

As she lay very still, thinking, she heard one of the girls — was it Nettie Periwinkle? — steal stealthily past her, but she made no sign. The figure, with its long wavy hair floating over the enveloping blanket, made its way noiselessly to the Pie, and hid a slim, perfumy letter deep down under the other things.

Only a letter, only a short letter, too. But there was a secret in it, the dearest secret a girl ever has, and thus confided with profoundest care to aunt Moneywort, first of all.

"Nobody else must even guess, yet," said the letter.

And now, till the bells of Christmas morning chimed from their high places glad greetings to the holy day, the discreet Pie stood alone, plump and patient, on the shining board, no whit discomposed by the responsibility of all the different trusts committed to its capacious bosom.

The wind rose and then fell away again, seeming to hold its breath in very surprise at the thousands of snowflakes that came down, at this hour, when nobody would be looking, and deftly dressed the old earth for Christmas Day in virgin white.

But within, now at length, only the old long clock staid awake and kept the Pie company with its stately ticking. What the Pie said to the Clock, and what the Clock said to the Pie, who can tell?

Often had the old Clock recalled the Past; could it also foretell the Future?

Had Maud been there to listen, could she have caught some hint of the wifely trust, not unlike that of her ancestress Agatha, which in time to come she would be capable of?

If cousin Red had been there, would she have learned too soon all that years had in store for her — love mixed with loss, pain out of which came new strength, effort and endurance that earned the victory which is far sweeter and far nobler than ease?

If Rite had been there, might she have heard the babbler tell of the old Albrey place in the country, where her father would be steward for many a happy year to come, and her mother grow strong and well?

But there was no need to know all this then. Rite herself would have said, if she had had the chance, "I would rather Providence should keep the other half, just as it did for mother in her story, until the right time."

And she would have been wise in saying so.

Therefore nobody ever tried to find out what the Pie said to the Clock, or what the Clock said to the Pie, in all those hours when they were left alone together.

THE END.

Little Folks' Every Day Book.

RYHMES AND ILLUSTRATIONS FOR EVERY DAY.

MAY 18TH.

A song of a nest : —

There was once a nest in a hollow ;

Down in the mosses and knot-grass pressed,

Soft and warm, and full to the brim:

MAY 19TH.

"Good night!" said the hen, when her
    supper was done,

  To Fanny who stood in the door,

"Good night," answered she, "come back
    in the morn,

  And you and your chicks shall have more."

MAY 20TH.

There's a merry brown thrush sitting up
  , in the tree,

"He's singing to me! He's singing to
  me !"

And what does he say, little girl, little boy ?

"Oh, the world's running over with joy"

Edited by AMANDA B. HARRIS.

TWELVE COLOR DESIGNS EMBLEMATIC OF THE MONTHS·
By GEORGE F. BARNES.

Square 18mo, tinted edges, $1 00.

D. LOTHROP & CO., Publishers, 30 and 32 Franklin St , Boston.

"PANSY" BOOKS.

Probably no living author has exerted an influence upon the American people at large, at all comparable with Pansy's. Thousands upon thousands of families read her books every week, and the effect in the direction of right feeling, right thinking, and right living is incalculable.

Each volume 12mo. Cloth. Price, $1.50.

FOUR GIRLS AT CHAUTAUQUA.
CHAUTAUQUA GIRLS AT HOME.
RUTH ERSKINE'S CROSSES.
ESTER RIED.
JULIA RIED.
KING'S DAUGHTER.
WISE AND OTHERWISE.
ESTER RIED "YET SPEAKING."
LINKS IN REBECCA'S LIFE.
FROM DIFFERENT STAND-
THREE PEOPLE.   [POINTS.
HOUSEHOLD PUZZLES.

MODERN PROPHETS.
ECHOING AND RE-ECHOING.
THOSE BOYS.
THE RANDOLPHS.
TIP LEWIS.
SIDNEY MARTIN'S CHRISTMAS.
DIVERS WOMEN.
A NEW GRAFT.
THE POCKET MEASURE.
MRS. SOLOMON SMITH.
THE HALL IN THE GROVE.
MAN OF THE HOUSE.

AN ENDLESS CHAIN.

Each volume 12mo. Cloth. Price, $1.25.

CUNNING WORKMEN.
GRANDPA'S DARLING.
MRS. DEAN'S WAY.
DR. DEAN'S WAY.

MISS PRISCILLA HUNTER and
    MY DAUGHTER SUSAN.
WHAT SHE SAID and
    PEOPLE WHO HAVEN'T TIME.

Each volume 16mo. Cloth. Price, $1.00.

NEXT THINGS.
PANSY SCRAP BOOK.
FIVE FRIENDS.

MRS. HARRY HARPER'S
    AWAKENING.
NEW YEAR'S TANGLES.

SOME YOUNG HEROINES.

Each volume 16mo. Cloth. Price, $.75.

GETTING AHEAD.
TWO BOYS.
SIX LITTLE GIRLS.
PANSIES.
THAT BOY BOB.

JESSIE WELLS.
DOCIA'S JOURNAL.
HELEN LESTER.
BERNIE'S WHITE CHICKEN.
MARY BURTON ABROAD.

SIDE BY SIDE. Price, $.60.

The Little Pansy Series, 10 vols. Boards, $3.00. Cloth, $4.00
Mother's Boys and Girls' Library, 12 vols. Quarto Boards, $3.00
Pansy Primary Library, 30 vol. Cloth. Price, $7.50.
Half Hour Library. Octavo, 8 vols. Price, $3.20.

The Yensie Walton Books.

These books, from the pen of Mrs. S. R. Graham Clark, are possessed of such conspicuous merits, as to secure for them the unqualified commendation of eminent religious journals such as the *Central Christian Advocate*, *The Journal and Messenger*, *The New Orleans Christian Advocate*, *The Lutheran Observer*, *Christian at Work*, The *Dover Morning Star*, *The Gospel Banner*, *Philadelphia Methodist*, *Herald and Presbyter*.

YENSIE WALTON. **OUR STREET.**
YENSIE WALTON'S WOMAMHOOD.
THE TRIPLE E. **ACHOR.**
12mo, cloth, illustrated, uniform binding, $1.50 each.

YENSIE WALTON.

"Yensie Walton," by Mrs. S. R. Graham Clark. Boston: D. Lothrop & Co. Full of striking incident and scenes of great pathos, with occasional gleams of humor and fun by way of relief to the more tragic parts of the narrative. The characters are strongly drawn, and, in general, are thoroughly human, not gifted with impossible perfections, but having those infirmities of the flesh which make us all akin. It will take rank among the best and most popular Sunday-school books. — *Episcopal Register*.

A pure sweet story of girl life, quiet, and yet of sufficient interest to hold the attention of the most careless reader. — *Zion's Advocate*.

YENSIE WALTON'S WOMANHOOD.

The many readers who have made the acquaintance of "Yensie Walton" in one of the best Sunday-school books ever published, will be delighted to renew that acquaintance, and to keep their former companion still further company through life. There is a strong religious tone to the whole story, and its teachings of morality and religion are pure and healthful and full of sweetness and beauty. The story is a worthy successor to Mrs. Clark's previous work. — *Boston Post*.

The heroine is an excellent character for imitation, and the entire atmosphere of the book is healthful and purifying. — *Pittsburg Christian Advocate*.

OUR STREET,

By the same author, is a capital story of every day life which deals with genuine character in a most interesting manner.

THE TRIPLE E,

Just published, is a book whose provoking title will be at once acknowledged by the reader as an appropriate one. It fully sustains the author's reputation.

ACHOR, a new book.

MARIE OLIVER'S STORIES.

3 vols, 12mo cloth, illustrated, $1.50 each; the set $4.50.

RUBY HAMILTON.   OLD AND NEW FRIENDS.
SEBA'S DISCIPLINE.

Extracts from comments of well-known journals.

RUBY HAMILTON.

This is a very excellent Sunday-school book, which can be honestly commended for youthful readers.—*The Watchman.*

It is a well-told story, conveys a pure, healthful lesson, and is one of the best books of its class.—*Philadelphia Enquirer.*

This is one of the best Sunday-school books in Lothrop's long and admirable list. The story is a sweet one, and charmingly told.—*Church Mirror.*

The spirit throughout is healthy and devout. . . . Altogether it is a charming and instructive book.—*The Churchman.*

OLD AND NEW FRIENDS.

A very excellent specimen of the class of fiction designed for young folk who have ceased to be children without having become mature men and women.—*N. Y. Evening Post.*

Many readers will remember "Ruby Hamilton," a volume which created quite a sensation at the time of its publication. . . . This volume, a continuation of this story, ought to become as popular as its predecessor.—*Christian Mirror.*

Contains some charming pictures of home-life. . . . Cannot but help and strengthen the boy whose impulses are for good.—*Herald and Presbyter.*

Like all that comes from this author's pen, this volume has merits of both substance and style.—*Western Christian Advocate.*

Adds another to the list of really good story books.—*Cincinnati Journal and Messenger.*

SEBA'S DISCIPLINE.

A good book to teach the uses of trouble in building up character.—*Western Recorder.*

Has a varied and absorbing interest from its beginning to its close. . . . Sometimes sad and wonderfully pathetic; sometimes bright and cheerful, it is impressive always. In every respect it is the best religious story we have seen for many a day, and one . . . that can scarcely fail to benefit any reader whom God leads along rough paths.—*The Interior.*

Should be in every Sunday-school library.—*The Standard.*

MARGARET SIDNEY'S BOOKS.

Margaret Sidney may be safely set down as one of the best writers of juvenile literature in the country. — *Boston Transcript.*

Margaret Sidney's books are happily described as "strong and pure from cover to cover, . . bright and piquan as the mountain breezes, or a dash on pony back of a June morning." The same writer speaks of her as "An American authoress who will hold her own in the competitive good work executed by the many bright writing women of to-day."

There are few better story writers than Margaret Sidney. — *Herald and Presbyter.*

Comments of the Secular and Religious Press.

FIVE LITTLE PEPPERS AND HOW THEY GREW.

A charming work. . . The home scenes in which these little Peppers are engaged are capitally described. . . Will find prominent place among the higher class of juvenile presentation books.—*Religious Herald.*

One of the best told tales given to the children for some time. . . The perfect reproduction of child-life in its minutest phases, catches one's attention at once. — *Christian Advocate.*

A good book to place in the hands of every boy or girl. — *Chicago Inter-Ocean.*

SO AS BY FIRE.

Will be hailed with eager delight, and found well worth reading.— *Christian Observer.*

An admirable Sunday-school book — *Arkansas Evangel.*

We have followed with intense interest the story of David Folsom. . . . A man poor, friendless, and addicted to drink; . . the influence of little Cricket; . . the faithful care of aunt Phebe; all steps by which he climbed to higher manhood. — *Woman at Work.*

THE PETTIBONE NAME.

It is one of the finest pieces of American fiction that has been published for some time. — *Newsdealers' Bulletin*, New York.

It ought to attract wide attention from the simplicity of its style, and the vigor and originality of its treatment. — *Chicago Herald.*

This is a capital story illustrating New England life. - *Inter-Ocean*, Chicago.

The characters of the story seem all to be studies from life. — *Boston Post.*

It is a New England tale, and its characters are true to the original type, and show careful study and no little skill in portraiture. — *Christian at Work*, New York.

To be commended to readers for excellent delineations, sparkling style, bright incident and genuine interest — *The Watchman.*

A capital story; bright with excellent sketches of character. Conveys good moral and spiritual lessons. . . In short, the book is in every way well done. *Illustrated Christian Weekly.*

HALF YEAR AT BRONCKTON.

A live boy writes: "This is about the best book that ever was written or ever can be."

"This bright and earnest story ought to go into the hands of every boy who is old enough to be subjected to the temptations of school life."